I0726927

Stories of the Veil

the UNVEILED

THE UNVEILED

STORIES OF THE VEIL

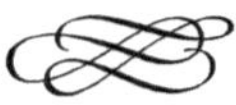

PEPPER MCGRAW

P
M
G
Publishing

CONTENTS

ASTRA

GLORY

ASTRA

CHAPTER 1

MORTAL SIDE OF THE WESTERN VEIL, LAWRENCE, KANSAS

Kahji Nenzele kept his back to the Veil and his eyes on the chaos of the battle around them.

The Veil hid Faerie from mortal eyes, but it was the shield Princess Astra had constructed around the Fae that concealed them.

Despite the shield, as Captain of the Royal Guard, Kahji didn't trust that things wouldn't go wrong in a heartbeat, especially when the college campus he'd expected was instead a battlefield overrun by mortals attacking one another.

The only good news was that none of the mortals appeared to be carrying swords.

Instead, they used their bodies as weapons, hurtling themselves at each other, hitting the ground and piling on top of one another before standing and beginning the process again.

It was the weirdest battle Kahji had ever seen. It seemed to move back and forth across the field in some strange pattern he couldn't quite discern.

In addition to the warriors on the field, Kahji also had to worry about the thousands of shouting mortals seated in tall structures on all four sides of them.

Kahji had a flash of memory from the far distant past: mortal gladiators, a giant colosseum, screaming spectators. It seemed the mortals had not changed much since the last time he had visited their realm.

At that moment, the mortal warriors all turned and barreled down the field toward them.

Kahji settled his hand on the hilt of his sword, ready to draw it should any of them manage to breach the shield Astra had constructed.

When they reached it, though, the runners blipped from one side to the other and continued running, seemingly unaware they had skipped an entire section of the field.

"Something's wrong," Astra exclaimed. "It's not working."

"What's not working?" Kahji winced as multiple warriors launched their bodies at another and they all went down in a pile of limbs.

"The Veil. It should have strengthened by now. It's

getting worse."

Kahji's attention snapped back to the Veil.

She was right.

The fractures in the Veil were spreading, rather than closing as usual. "Perhaps the Guardians haven't sealed themselves to it yet."

"No. They *have*. Something's wrong."

As if in response to her statement, the ground trembled beneath them and a white light exploded from the Veil, lighting up the field and sending all the warriors there, both Fae and mortal, to the ground.

Kahji woke to a silence that blanketed the world.

He struggled to his knees and crawled to Princess Astra's side.

Her eyes snapped open. "It's down," she whispered.

"What is?"

"The Veil."

For the second time that day, Kahji's attention snapped to the Veil, or at least to where it should have been.

The doorway to Faerie was still there, but this time, there was no Veil shielding Faerie from mortal eyes.

Kahji leapt to his feet, then reached down and pulled Astra to hers.

A quick glance around them revealed that Astra's shield was down as well.

This was not good.

The doorway to Faerie was clearly exposed, providing *thousands* of mortals, both warriors on the field and spectators in the seats above, a view of Faerie few of their kind had ever seen.

Worse yet, the Fae's glamour had fallen, unveiling their true forms to the mortals.

Astra fairly glowed with the magic of Faerie, causing the mortals to fall silent at the sight of her.

"I can't access my magic, Kahji," Astra muttered.

"I know. I can't either."

"Without our glamour, we're completely exposed out here."

A man dressed in a black and white shirt, shoved to the front of the mortal warriors and stormed toward Kahji and Astra, shouting, "What do you think you're doing, interrupting the game like that? Get off the field!"

"We can't do that, Kahji, not with Faerie exposed like this."

"Guardians!" Kahji shouted. "Defend the Princess and guard the entrance to Faerie!"

The Royal Guard scrambled into position. Four Guardians surrounded the doorway to Faerie while Dyranel and Zanzor joined Kahji at Astra's side.

All seven of the Royal Guard drew their swords and pointed them at the mortals.

Kahji nudged the princess backward toward the Veil

and snapped at the mortals advancing on them, "Stand back."

Astra ignored Kahji and called to the mortals, "You need to stop," then muttered to Kahji, "They aren't armed. Don't do anything rash."

"Armed or not, they're still warriors and there are too many of them at that. The seven of us cannot possibly hold back the tide. You need to return to Faerie at once."

At that moment, an entire unit of Fae Guardians poured in from Faerie. Three of them joined Astra and Kahji and the rest spread out in a protective circle around the doorway.

"We cannot leave the entrance to Faerie unprotected this side of the Veil," Astra said. "And I'm not leaving a single Fae behind, especially when our glamour has failed and we can't seem to tap into the magic of Faerie."

"Astra." Exasperation filled Kahji's voice. "Things are going to get ugly fast."

"I'm *not* leaving."

The sound of sirens filled the air and a few moments later, mortals Astra recognized as their version of Guardians stormed across the field toward them.

She was afraid Kahji was right. Things were about to get ugly.

Then it happened.

The Veil came up with an almost-audible pop. For one second, Astra couldn't breathe as the Veil drew energy from every Fae present to form anew.

A quick glance at the mortals, then back to the Veil, and Astra knew it was still not shielding Faerie from mortal eyes. Instead—she brushed up against the Veil with her magic and instantly understood that none of them would be going home anytime soon.

The Veil had solidified into a transparent shield that protected Faerie from anyone crossing into its lands, including the Fae now locked in the mortal realm.

The only good news was that with the Veil's return, Astra now had access to the magic of Faerie and her own power once more.

The mortal Guardian force, who had faltered at the sight of the many Fae with swords drawn and once more at the sight of the doorway to Faerie, recovered and surged forward.

"Put down your weapons," a mortal Guardian shouted even as his entire force pointed *their* weapons at the Fae.

Astra sighed.

Really.

Could nothing be simple anymore?

Kahji let out a growl of true anger and stepped in front of her, shielding her from the mortals' weapons.

That simple movement set off a chain reaction of events.

A popping sound filled the air and Kahji let out a grunt as he was flung backward into Astra.

They both fell to the ground as more pops sounded and a mortal shouted, "Hold your fire. Hold your fire!"

As the Fae realized they were under attack, they moved swiftly to surround their wounded and began wielding their swords as shields, pinging tiny pieces of metal back toward the mortals who were attacking them.

"Enough!" Astra shoved her magic outward in a huge surge of power.

Lightning rippled across the field, freezing mortals and Fae alike.

She struggled from beneath Kahji and saw that blood was pouring outward from where he'd fallen in a spreading lake of Fae power.

She let out a scream of pure rage and flung her power into that lake, lifting each tiny droplet of blood upward.

Her power caught Kahji in its grip and brought him back to standing.

The droplets of blood flowed back into the multiple wounds in his shoulder, chest and thigh.

The bullets that had exited his flesh ripped free from the ground and a wooden post twenty feet behind where Kahji and Astra had been standing and traveled their pathway backwards, sliding through Kahji's form, flesh and bone knitting behind them, as they returned to the weapons from which they had been fired.

As Astra's power wrapped around Kahji's form, he was lifted higher into the air, the bright light of her magic lighting up his form.

The sight of him still unconscious fueled Astra's fury. The lighting whip of her power whirled around the field in ever-increasing surges, intensified by rage and pain and fear.

That power yanked mortal weapons from the hands of the men and women who held them, crushing those weapons to dust in seconds.

"We are the Fae," she roared as she stormed away from where Kahji still hovered mid-air, his form still blanketed in the healing waves of her power.

Those waves spread ever outward, first covering the other Fae who had been felled by those same pieces of metal that had wounded Kahji, then covering those mortals who had fallen when the Fae had deflected their weapons back toward them.

"We are the Fae," she repeated, her voice echoing

across the field and into the stands where many mortals still sat, frozen in silence as they watched the confrontation on the field below. "We do not yield to mortals. We do not fall at your feet just because you wish it to be so. We are the immortal Fae and as is our right, by virtue of the Fae blood spilt upon these lands, we now claim them for the Fae."

She used her power to lift every mortal on the field, wounded and not, and began to move them farther and farther away from her fallen Fae warriors.

Her power stretched outward, sweeping up the mortals in the stands all around her, carrying them out of the stadium in every direction and leaving them, frozen and silent on its perimeter.

As the stands emptied of mortals, she sent another contraction of her power whipping through, lightning-fast, compressing and disintegrating the entire structure in seconds.

Her power then whipped across the field, disintegrating everything unnatural in its path. Boards, signs, lampposts, flashing lights, everything that wasn't part of the living earth compressed into dust.

She stopped in the center of the field and turned in a circle, eyeing the mortals she had dropped at the edges of where their stadium had once stood.

She settled the mortal Guardians and the warriors who had been playing their game on the field just outside where the stadium's screen had once stood, on the far opposite end from where her warriors recovered from their wounds.

She glared at the mortal warriors, fury still a bright burn in her blood.

The mortals stood silent in every direction, all of them still wrapped in her power, frozen in stillness and silenced by it.

She let the moments stretch, one after the other, giving the mortals time to reflect on their powerlessness in the grip of the Fae, before finally pulling her power back.

As it slowly contracted away from the mortals, she shaped it into a giant shield that snapped into position where the stands had once stood, forming a barrier around land the Fae would never again yield to the mortals.

When the shield settled into place, she rose into the air and glared down at the mortal Guardians who were still frozen and silent, though they had been released from her power. "We have shown you mercy. The power of Faerie has healed every mortal injured by the foolishness of your own Guardian force. Do not make the mistake of believing we will show you that same mercy again, for I assure you, we will not. Go home now. This land we have claimed for the Fae."

Astra.

*K*ahji's entire form was engulfed in heat. He could feel her essence burning through every fiber of his being, prying open that pathway he'd sealed off eleven hundred years before.

He came back to the world fully erect, on fire for the Fae he had loved throughout eternity.

Astra.

She hovered high above the field that still crackled in the wake of her fire.

White lightning zipped across the field and up into the sky, traveling a path in reverse, surging from the land beneath them, wrapping everything he could see in its embrace.

He shuddered in the grip of an endless, burning need as she turned to face him, her gorgeous blue eyes shining bright in the falling twilight.

Astra.

Kahji?

The stunned wonder in her voice brought him back to his senses.

He shut down the pathway with a flick of his magic, acting out of both instinct and habit.

He struggled to tamp down his raging desire, to

prepare for the monumental effort of pretending these last few magical moments had never happened.

Having heard her voice in his head, something he'd never thought a possibility—having felt her magic in his blood and his veins, stroking across his skin—he wasn't certain he would succeed in that endeavor.

Indeed, it was quite possible he would go mad with the effort of continuing to deny their bond.

Still. He had to try.

Princess Astra was not for the likes of him.

The minute she heard his voice, Astra lost all interest in the foolish mortals.

She was turning toward him when she heard his voice again.

Astra.

With a sense of wonder and anticipation, she responded, *Kahji?*

No response.

He was where she'd left him, hovering mid-air on the other side of the field, far from where she'd taken the mortals. His eyes were on her, though, and she thought, even from this distance, that the way he looked at her in that moment was entirely new.

Then, his eyes shuttered and he was back to the Fae she knew: Captain of the Royal Guard and Royal Pain in her Arse.

"Astra," he shouted. "Get back here right now and let me down from here!"

She rolled her eyes, settled back on the ground and allowed the rest of her power, the lightning that still whipped across the field in increasingly smaller waves, to dissipate.

She strolled calmly toward Kahji as her power deposited him back on his feet and he surged toward her, the rest of the Royal Guard rushing in his wake.

Overprotective as usual.

The Guard surrounded her and Kahji launched into one of his favorite pastimes: lecturing her.

Most of it she had heard many times before, though there was the occasional new twist.

"You know you are not to leave the Guard's presence when we are traveling."

Never mind that the entire Guard had either been down or under attack.

"A princess does not ever show such a blatant overuse of power."

Never mind that her "blatant overuse of power" had ended the confrontation and healed the wounded.

"I cannot believe you would place yourself at such

risk, revealing your power to the mortals and exposing the Fae."

Now *that* she took extreme exception to. "Excuse me! I did *not* expose the Fae. The Veils fell and I assure you, I had nothing to do with that."

"Yes." Kahji glowered across the field at the unit of Guardians who stood near the Veil, prepared as always to defend it. "I know *exactly* who is responsible for that." He took off toward the Guardians of the Veil.

Astra hurried after him, worried that he might actually harm the Guardians they now needed more than ever.

"Explain to me exactly how this happened," Kahji shouted.

Kalina Wyendeh stepped forward, her mate, Thorne Evaria at her side.

"How could you fail in your one sacred duty to the Fae?" Kahji demanded.

"We have no idea what happened," Kalina said.

"We followed all of the rituals exactly," Thorne said.

Another Guardian of the Veil—Astra thought his name was Mitaru—stepped forward. "We did have two Guardians fall five weeks before the ceremonies. They were replaced by someone from the Reserves and by Thorne, who is an experienced Guardian from the East."

"I'm aware," Astra spoke quickly before Kahji could

start yelling again. "I do not believe such minor changes could possibly have had this impact." She eyed Kalina and Thorne. "Perhaps, though, a mated pair made all the difference."

Kalina blanched. "You think our mating caused this?"

"That was not our intent," Thorne said, a stricken look on his face.

"Your mating was blessed by the Fae Queen herself," Astra said. "This was not anticipated by any of us. The seers insisted Thorne needed to be at the Western Veil and that resulted in your mating. Given those facts, I cannot see how this could be anything other than the guiding hand of fate.

"But none of this matters right now. Not when we are locked in the mortal world, unable to return to Faerie, unveiled to mortal eyes."

"Our glamour is back," Kalina said. "We should be able to veil ourselves again, at least. Right?"

"Unfortunately, Fae glamour does not work on mortal eyes that have seen and accepted the truth," Kahji said.

"Then we should wipe their memories," Thorne said.

"It is too late for that," Astra said. "There were recording devices everywhere. We are well and truly unveiled."

CHAPTER 2

Four weeks in the mortal realm. *Four weeks.*

It was more than enough time to make any Fae go mad.

This was what Kahji kept thinking as he watched Princess Astra storm around the room, throwing things at him and shouting.

He'd gone mad.

It was the only explanation.

Centuries he'd kept this secret from her.

Not even once tempted to tell her the truth.

Well, maybe once.

Or twice.

A day.

But never had he actually done it!

Yet trap him for four weeks in the mortal realm and

apparently he went mad, blurting out the truth just because she asked for it.

Madness.

The rest of the Guard had all abandoned him to his fate.

Something he would have claimed was impossible.

If anyone had asked, he would have said the Guard he served with would never abandon him on the field of battle.

He would have been wrong though.

They couldn't flee fast enough.

The cowards.

He might have laughed at the looks on their faces when they realized what he'd admitted, but he'd been entirely too busy worrying about Astra's response to the news.

"I cannot believe you!" Astra shrieked.

Kahji sighed. This wasn't the first time she'd said this.

He stepped to the side and winced at the sound of the vase she'd hurled at his head breaking against the wall behind him.

He was actually quite relieved she was finally yelling. When he'd first admitted the truth, that they were mates and he'd known for centuries, she'd gone deadly silent.

The type of silence that usually signaled an impending death.

As he'd been sure it was his death she'd been plotting, he'd been quite relieved when an hour into the seething silence, she'd exploded into motion and starting throwing things and shouting at him.

By the fates, she was terrifying.

It took all his discipline as a Fae warrior not to claim her right then.

*A*stra could barely think.

She'd had a crush on the captain of her Royal Guard for as long as she could remember.

Centuries she'd wanted him.

But the pathway between mates hadn't opened when they'd met for the first time. She hadn't worried then, for she'd been under the age of majority.

She'd waited, longing for her hundredth birthday, absolutely certain that the moment they saw each other on that day, the path would open and they would claim each other as mates.

When her birthday came and went and nothing changed, she'd been devastated.

Until that moment, she'd worshipped Kahji,

following wherever he led, complying with his every demand, adoring him as only a child could.

When she'd realized the man she adored wasn't her fated mate, she'd spiraled downward. It had taken her another hundred years to recover her joy, to finally accept that some other Fae, not Kahji, was her destined mate.

She'd thrown herself into the search, dragging her Royal Guard all over Faerie, meeting as many Fae as she could, flirting with them all, driving Kahji mad, guarding her heart and pretending he wasn't still the love of her life.

And now, *eleven hundred years* past her majority, he was finally admitting they were mates?

It made no sense. He should *never* have been able to shield that truth from her.

Her rage waned as her brain kicked in and she began to think once more.

Of course, that didn't stop her from using her magic to launch yet another book at his egotistical, arrogant, *lying* head.

"Astra. Love. Let me explain."

"*Explain?* As if there could be any explanation for this."

"You were young when we met."

"Not that young! I was seventy-six years old, you pompous ass!"

"Entirely too young to become mate to someone approaching his two thousandth birthday."

This *again*. Always this. Like two thousand years made him ancient when those years were merely a drop in the vast oceanic lifespan of a Fae. "And what's your excuse for the *last* thousand years?"

"Even when you reached your majority, you were still so young. You hadn't had the opportunity to discover who you were. You looked at me with stars in your eyes."

Astra could feel herself blushing. "Well, don't worry. There aren't any stars anymore." She glared at him.

Kahji nodded. "That's good. You needed time to grow up."

"A thousand years?" she demanded dryly. "How did you manage it anyway?"

He sighed. "When mates meet and one is over the age of majority and the other is not, it's tradition for the one who is older to use magic to hold their pathway closed to keep the younger one's development from being influenced by the older one. You know this."

"Of course I do and I support that. Children have the right to grow into adulthood as individuals before being dragged into a mating. That doesn't mean you get to keep the pathway closed forever! I expected you to open it when I hit my majority. That you didn't—I thought that meant we weren't mates. You broke my heart, Kahji."

At least she was finally talking to him, but hearing the pain in her voice, seeing the tears shining in her eyes, he wasn't sure she would ever forgive him.

By the fates, he'd made a mess of things.

He struggled for the right words, to somehow help her understand without hurting her worse than he already had. "I'm sorry, Astra, but you weren't ready. You would never have become the woman you are today—the strong princess, the potential Queen—if I had claimed you back then. You needed time to grow into your sense of self, into your *power.*"

"As the mortals would say, *what a load of crock.* I might accept that answer if you'd only kept this from me for the first hundred years. Maybe even two hundred years. But for *eleven hundred* years, Kahji? Even I couldn't possibly take that long to mature."

"That's not what I meant, Astra, and you know it. I should have told you long ago, but the truth is allowing you the time to become who you were meant to be was a double-edged sword. You're amazing, Astra, in every way, and the more time that passed, the more I realized how unworthy of you I truly am."

For a second, Astra just stared at him, apparently speechless, then she shrieked, "Unworthy? You're the Captain of my Guard, for fate's sake! You've risked your life countless times, most recently taking mortal bullets to protect me. How could you possibly think you're unworthy?"

Before Kahji could reply, a throat clearing caught their attention. "Ah, Kahji, Astra, sorry to interrupt."

"What is it, Andri?" Kahji asked.

"The mortals are back. They claim to have papers that give them the right to force us off this land."

"Seriously?" Astra demanded. "I just can't even. These mortals are the bane of my existence. Stubborn, idiotic, self-righteous, hypocritical *thieves*! Do they think we do not know their history of land-snatching? Ugh. I am so done with this conversation."

Kahji just shook his head. "I told you they weren't going to accept, no matter how many times you eject them. They want these lands and they're not giving them up."

"I shouldn't have stopped at Mississippi Street. It just gave them ideas, like I wasn't serious when I said I would burn the rest of their territories to the ground if they kept coming back." She stormed past Andri and out the front door, tossing over her shoulder, "And don't think for a minute this conversation is over, Kahji. We're just getting started!"

"*W*as that really necessary?" Kahji demanded two hours later as he followed Astra back into her rooms.

Astra rolled her eyes, not at all surprised at his response. "Perhaps not, but I'm done trying to negotiate with these mortals."

"I'm sorry. I must have misunderstood. Are you saying that was a *negotiation?*"

"Of *course* it was a negotiation! I told them we weren't giving back the lands and they refused to listen, so I *made* them listen."

"Huh. It appears our definitions of *negotiate* are quite different."

"As the mortals would say, *whatever.* Now let's get back to this whole mate conversation. Explain to me again exactly *why* I had to wait more than *one thousand years* to find out you're my *mate!*" Astra was shrieking by the end, but she just couldn't help it.

The entire time she'd been with the mortals, *negotiating,* she'd been stewing over her memories of a thousand years of believing Kahji wasn't her mate: how brokenhearted she'd been in the beginning, the years she'd wasted searching for a mate she'd already met, the unsatiated hunger she'd felt whenever in his presence and how she'd struggled to tamp it down year after year after year.

A thousand years of agony and for what? So that he could claim he wasn't good enough for her?

It was completely outrageous, insufferable, maddening and absolutely *infuriating*.

"Astra. You could easily ascend to Queen one day."

"Bite your tongue! You know that Zivek will be King one day, which means his mate shall be queen."

"Unless something happens to him or he chooses not to ascend."

"Should that happen, one of my other brothers would ascend instead, and their mate would be queen." Thank goodness. Astra regularly gave thanks to the fates that they had seen fit to provide her with three older brothers who would take on the realm if need be. "I have no desire to be queen and you know it."

"I'm just saying it could happen, and Astra, whether you think so or not, you would make an excellent queen."

"Aw, that's sweet." Astra gave him her most insincere smile, then snarled, "But it still doesn't explain why we didn't mate *eleven hundred years ago*!"

"I'm a Guardian, Astra. It's what I do. I serve

Faerie and her Royal families. I fight when I need to fight and I will die if need be to protect those under my care. I am not meant to be king of the realm."

"And I'm not meant to be queen. I'm pretty sure we just established that. But if, in some nightmare alternate realm, I had to ascend, I would do so for the good of Faerie, and *so would you.*

"You just said it yourself, Kahji. You will fight and die to protect Faerie and all those under your care. Well, we Fae have a long history of Warrior Kings and Queens serving, then dying for Faerie. You and I, we would be no different." She glared at him, not certain what else to say to convince him, not even certain she *wanted* to convince him.

Why was she even trying? He clearly didn't want her. "Forget it. Obviously, you're not interested and that's fine."

"What? No. Astra—"

"It's fine." It infuriated Astra to hear the slight tremble in her voice. "I have to go. We'll talk more later."

"Astra —"

She ignored him and walked out.

He'd never lied to her before, but he was one of the most respected Guardians of the realm. How could he believe he wasn't worthy?

And did she want to try and convince him otherwise?

It had taken her weeks to come up with the courage to ask Kahji outright if he was hers.

In eleven hundred years, it had never occurred to her to ask because it had never occurred to her that he would willfully deprive them both of their destined mate. Then she'd heard his voice inside her head the day the Veils fell, and everything had changed.

She'd initially planned to ask him immediately, but they were so busy in the beginning, trying to figure out how to survive in this mortal realm, that she'd decided to wait until things calmed down a bit.

Once they had, it had still taken her days to figure out exactly what she wanted to say, then still more days to gather her courage to ask something no Fae should ever have to.

Because they should just *know*.

After eleven hundred years of believing they weren't mates, Astra knew that regardless of whether the answer was yes or no, she would always feel foolish for having asked the question.

And so, that morning, feeling a nauseating mix of hope and shame, she'd blurted out, "Kahji, tell me the truth. Are we mates?"

She hadn't even waited until they were alone. She'd wanted to be able to quiz the other Guardians if he denied it. She'd wanted witnesses who could tell her whether they thought he was speaking the truth or not.

He'd frozen in such a way, though, that she'd known, witnesses or no, he *was* her mate.

He'd looked at her with that look in his eyes, the one she'd seen on the field that day, filled with a blazing heat and a desire that had threatened to send her entire body up in flames.

Then he'd blinked and that Fae was gone, replaced by the typical, aloof, judgmental, *bossy* Captain of her Royal Guard and she'd just *known* he was going to lie.

"Don't lie," she'd snapped at him. "Tell me the truth, Kahji. *Are we mates?*"

He'd dragged in a deep breath and said, so softly she almost didn't hear the words, "We are."

The rest of the Fae had frozen the moment she'd asked the question and for one long moment after he'd answered, they'd remained frozen, as did she, then they'd all bolted for the door.

She'd simply stared at Kahji, ignoring the other Fae, lost in her memories of heartbreak and devastating loneliness.

She'd seethed, vibrating in fury, then eventually had exploded with it.

He hadn't tried to defend himself, though he had tried to explain, but she hadn't listened because eleven hundred years of memories were a roar in her ears that drowned out everything else.

She should probably let him explain again and this time really listen to the words, to the emotions beneath them.

But not yet.

Not today.

After all, she had suffered for eleven hundred years, believing he wasn't her mate.

He could definitely endure her wrath a bit longer.

CHAPTER 3

THREE DAYS LATER

"It was a mistake to send away half the Guardians of the Veil." Kahji paced from one side of the courtyard to the other, flowers and blades of grass straining away from his boots as he passed.

Astra ignored him, focused instead on the tiny, iridescent hummingbird that had come to rest on her finger. So beautiful, so fragile, so extraordinarily fast.

The hummingbird took off, zipping to a flower, its movements almost too quick for even a Fae's eye to catch.

"Come on, Astra," Kahji said, exasperation clear in his tone. "You can't ignore me forever."

Actually, she could.

Besides, she was tired of this argument.

Not that they'd actually argued.

More like Kahji had yelled and lectured and paced and Astra had ignored him.

When he'd finally run out of energy and things to say, she'd turned to Kalina and ordered her to take half her unit to the east.

Basically, Astra had done something she rarely did: she'd pulled rank.

And enjoyed it.

Kahji had stewed and glowered as Kalina had gathered her unit and identified who would go with her and who would stay.

Of course, she'd immediately identified her best friend, Mitaru, and her mate, Thorne, as two who would accompany her.

Something that Kahji had also had much to say about.

He'd ranted that at least one of the three should remain with Astra, but both Astra and Kalina had overridden him, which had just made him angrier.

Kalina had ridden out with half her unit, just an hour before, and Kahji had been growling about it ever since.

"They even took all the horses. It took Rashideh and Lumina weeks to acquire those mortal beasts and now we have no means of transportation yet again."

Like the Guardians hadn't enjoyed using their magic

to travel all over the midwest, tracking down the fastest and strongest steeds available.

Like they wouldn't enjoy doing it again.

"Astra, come on. We can't go on like this. I'm the Captain of your Guard." Damn him for sounding so calm and reasonable. "Just talk to me, *please*."

Grrr.

She hated it when he did that.

Made her feel like a child holding a grudge.

"Fine," she snapped, pulling her attention from the hummingbird to glare at him, refusing to be moved by the look of sheer relief on his face. "Glory needs the Guard more than we do. No one's seen her since the Veils fell and I'm worried about her."

"I know you are, Astra, but your sister can take care of herself. Her magic is a lot more offensive than yours. Besides, according to that interweb thing, she had many more Guardians at her side than we did here. The majority of *our* forces were delayed by the Sorenalaya and trapped inside Faerie, whereas Guardians literally *poured* through the Eastern Veil to protect Glory. With that many Guardians at her side, I'm sure she's fine."

"Then why haven't we heard from her? Why has no one seen her since the cameras went dark? Why did the mortal government shut down all communications from D.C.?"

Kahji sighed. "I have no idea."

"Well, I do. She's in trouble. I can feel it. While the mortals here have more or less accepted our presence—"

Kahji let out a snort of derision.

"Okay, fine, but progress is definitely—possibly, kind of—being made. At least I know we're safe behind our shield, whereas we have no idea what is happening in D.C. because they're not communicating. No news has come out of that city in four weeks and the last sight I had of my sister was of her being surrounded by entire troops of well-armed, hostile mortals. Obviously, she needed the Guard more than I did, but I still kept half of them, didn't I?"

"You did and I appreciate it, but Astra, you can't be naive. These mortals aren't our friends. They want this land back and they want us gone."

"Well, they can't have it back, now can they? I believe I've made that quite clear."

In fact, Astra had lost her temper on a couple memorable occasions as the police officers she'd ejected that first day in the mortal realm were replaced by something called the National Guard and then by increasing numbers of mortals who only ever identified themselves with initials—the FBI, the CIA and the NSA, to name a few.

Each confrontation, she'd claimed more land for the

Fae, ejecting the interlopers with the same vast display of power as before.

"You *have* made it clear. However, I'm finding it difficult to reconcile your behavior with the fact that you're supposed to be our *diplomatic* Princess," Kahji said dryly.

Astra whirled and glared at him. "What did you expect me to do?"

"I don't know. Enter into diplomatic conversations. Negotiate with the mortals."

"*Negotiate?* They opened fire and you were bleeding immortal blood everywhere, Kahji. You and Mitaru and seven others were down in seconds. If the magic of Faerie hadn't returned to us, if my magic wasn't primarily life magic, we would have lost all nine of you, right then. And what do you think would have happened next, Kahji?"

Kahji sighed. "Right. So diplomacy wasn't exactly an option when we were first unveiled, but you haven't even tried since then. It's been four weeks, Astra, and all you've been doing is flexing your power every time the mortals come around."

"Because they don't want to negotiate. They're as arrogant as they ever were and I'm waiting until they approach with a bit of humility, something they have yet to do."

"The problem is with every flex of your power, their determination not to yield just grows."

"Yes, well, *their* problem is every time they force me to flex it, *I get angrier.*"

Astra had never truly understood the phrase "blinding rage" until that terrible moment when she'd first seen Kahji lying so still on the ground, blood spreading beneath him, eyes closed, moments from death. In that moment, every mortal in the vicinity, possibly even the world, had been in terrible danger, for she had wanted them all to *burn.*

Now, every time the mortals demanded she return their lands, she flashed back to that moment—to how still he'd been, to the knowledge of how close she'd come to losing him and worse, to losing him without truly understanding the depths of that loss—and it took everything in her to restrain the darker side of her magic, a darker side she would have sworn didn't even exist six weeks ago.

Rather than give into that darkness each time, Astra instead calmly reminded the mortals that the Fae had taken the lands in payment for the blood the mortals had shed, and then she claimed yet more lands, because *obviously* they hadn't yet learned their lesson.

"Did you really have to surround the entire city with your forest?" Kahji demanded.

Astra shrugged. "I asked the magic where it wanted

to go. It was as impatient as me. Clearly grabbing a couple acres at a time wasn't making enough of an impression. The magic wanted what it wanted."

"And you had nothing to do with it."

Truthfully, Astra had lost patience with the mortals, but she wasn't going to admit that. "Well, I suppose I did, but you know how my magic is. It's *life* magic, completely intertwined with the magic of Faerie, and it's not easy to control. It wants what it wants and ever since we arrived here, all that it wants is to heal this land. *All* of these lands. It's hard to reign in, especially when I know that yielding back these lands would be reinstating their death sentence."

Kahji didn't speak for a moment. When he did, his voice was quiet. "Sometimes late at night, I can hear them screaming."

"I hear them all the time, Kahji, and I now believe with everything in me that *this* is why we Fae were called here. Like it or not, the lands of Faerie *are* connected to the lands of this earth, and if *they* die, it will not be long before Faerie follows."

Kahji nodded. "You're right. I just have to wonder. How did we not realize things had deteriorated to this extent?"

"Because we're as bad as the mortals, Kahji. We only care about our own interests and we've had no real interests on the mortal side of the Veils for millennia.

We may travel here occasionally, but no Fae has stayed long enough to realize how interconnected our lands really are, and now we're all paying the price for our stupidity and selfishness.

"So yes. Building the forest *was* necessary. It was a message to the mortals, but it was also a critical first step in protecting Faerie."

Because the healthier the mortal lands surrounding the doorways were, the healthier the lands of Faerie would be. In a way, the mortals' refusal to accept their new reality was a boon for Faerie because it gave Astra an excuse to continually push the boundaries of the lands they had claimed.

This latest confrontation, though, had ended Astra's patience with the mortals and the games they played.

She was done with making her point through tiny incremental, boundary shifts, and instead, had sent her magic rippling underground throughout the entire city of Lawrence.

Giant slabs of concrete and asphalt had cracked beneath the spreading roots of her magic. Flowers and trees had bloomed everywhere.

Vines had sprouted from the ground, overtaking houses and buildings, lampposts and electrical towers.

Lights had flickered all over Lawrence and the interweb, as Kahji called it, had died, and for a moment, the entire city had gone dark. But then the magic of

Faerie had absorbed the intent of the technological grid of Lawrence and everything had come back.

The Fae now not only had access to the mortal web, but they had their own Fae web as well, and their access was not confined to tiny devices like it was for the mortals.

The Fae could now access the web on any flat surface with just a tiny bit of concentration and magic.

They had succeeded in connecting with the Guardians of the Northern Veil just the day before and had connected to those of the Southern Veil the day before that.

It was their inability, though, to connect with those of the Eastern Veil that had led Astra to send half her Guardians to find and protect Glory.

"I still don't like it," Kahji said.

Astra knew he wasn't speaking of the forest or protecting faerie. Instead, without any warning or change in subject, he had returned them to the conversation about the Guardians of the Veil, making Astra realize how often he did that. Despite never acknowledging their bond, he constantly accessed it, even if only to subconsciously align their conversations with her thoughts.

"We don't have enough Guardians here in Lawrence to truly hold these lands, not if the mortals decide to wage war."

"We have plenty of Guardians for that, Kahji."

"We do not. Did you see how many mortals were in the stands? We are outnumbered, literally thousands to one."

"Which is why I built the forest and created a secondary shield."

When Astra's magic had reached the edges of Lawrence, leaving all of the lands of Lawrence blanketed in its power, she'd built the forest around the perimeter, then another shield to encompass everything, effectively cutting Lawrence off from the rest of the world.

"In another week or so, I'll create a pathway through the woods."

"Just one?" Kahji asked dryly.

Astra sighed. "Fine. Two. I'll make a path on the eastern side and another on the western side, but just because I'm going to give the mortals a couple points of entry and exit doesn't mean the woods will let them in."

"What in all the fates does that mean?" Kahji demanded.

"Look, it's not my fault the magic of Faerie has its own ideas about how to heal these lands. It's changing them and there's nothing we can do about it. Even if I create paths through the woods, there's no guarantee the trees will allow the mortals through. If the trees judge them unworthy, they will simply become lost and the forest will spit them back out on the mortal side of the woods once more."

Kahji just stared at her. "You grew a Judicia Forest here, on the mortal side of the Veils?"

Astra hesitated. "I'm not sure *grew* is the right word. I think the forests of Faerie sent their roots here. The forest was already waiting underground when my magic reached the edges of Lawrence. At that point, the trees just *exploded* into being."

"That shouldn't even be possible."

"And yet, that's what happened."

"Are you even in control of your magic, Astra?"

"As much as I ever am. I've told you before—*it wants what it wants.*"

Kahji groaned. "So basically, the answer is no. You're *not* in control."

Astra rolled her eyes.

She had no idea why Kahji was so obsessed with control.

It was always, "A princess must maintain control at all times," and never, "Losing control can be wonderfully fun in the right circumstances."

"This is not what we need to be worrying about right now, Kahji. It's time for us to step out into the mortal world and make our presence known."

"I think we've managed that quite well enough already, and in fact, have made any number of enemies as a result. We need to stay here, safely behind the shield, until the Veils open again and we can go home."

Astra shook her head. "That isn't going to happen, Kahji, not anytime soon. We're here for a reason and until that reason is met, the Veils won't let us back into Faerie."

"And how do you know that?"

"I just do. We have to actually participate in our destinies if we're going to meet them."

"You can meet your destiny just fine right here behind the shield of Faerie."

"Or not. Kahji, come on. It's time to step out of this bubble we're living in."

Kahji raised an eyebrow, then turned and stared at the castle behind them. "Some bubble."

"We needed shelter and I'm quite aware of the mortals' stories of the Fae. Little flying things who live in fairy tale castles. Well, we can't fly and we don't have wings and we're certainly not the size of insects, but I could give them a castle, so I did."

Astra had never used her magic to build something so elaborate before. She had needed not just life magic, but an incredible amount of earth magic as well. It had been exhausting and fun, first coaxing the land to rise into a hillside that could become home to the Fae, then tunneling it out and shaping it into elaborate rooms built into the landscape.

All of the Guardians had helped and the end result was truly magnificent: a castle made entirely of the living earth.

The roof was made of vines that shielded the structure in inclement weather and retreated when the weather was nice.

The furnishings were made of living trees that adjusted and moved according to the needs of the Fae at any given time.

The entire site had become a bit of a tourist attraction for some mortals and a place to protest for others. Of course, they had to do all their admiring and protesting from outside the primary shield Astra had constructed.

"I don't think a castle, no matter how pretty, is going to make up for destroying the mortals' stadium. They're still quite angry about it, Astra, and it's not like you built the castle for them. It's *our* castle. All *they* can do is look at it from afar and stew over the fact that it isn't their precious football stadium."

Astra let out a huff of exasperation. "I have no idea why these mortals are so obsessed with a game. You would think they would be grateful. After all, we're saving their land, healing it for generations to come."

"Yeah, I don't think they care about that, at least not as much as they care about football."

"Foolish mortals."

"Astra, there's a mortal at the edge of the shield, demanding to speak with you." Toren, one of Kalina's unit left behind, poked his head in to say.

"What does the mortal want?"

"He refuses to say."

Astra rolled her eyes. "Fine. Let's go see what new and interesting thing the mortals have to share today."

"Now, Astra, let's not do anything rash." Kahji hurried to catch up with her. "We need a new strategy since you've pretty much claimed the entirety of Lawrence at this point."

"Princess Astra!"

A man stood just outside the primary shield.

Of course, that meant he was *inside* the secondary one.

That was definitely going to be a problem.

The trees surrounding Lawrence would certainly refuse entry to any mortals they judged unworthy, but they could do nothing about the worthless ones already *inside* the shield.

The mortal waved an arm at her, papers fluttering in his hand.

"You've been served!" He shouted, then flung his hand wide.

The papers he'd been clutching flew across the field, then fell to the ground.

Astra rolled her eyes. "Am I supposed to know what that means?"

"I think you're supposed to collect the papers," Kahji said, "though I'm not sure why you'd want to."

When none of the Fae moved, the mortal shrugged his shoulders, turned and walked away.

"Do you want me collect them?" Toren asked. "Just in case?"

Astra grinned. "Absolutely. If nothing else, they should prove quite entertaining."

CHAPTER 4

"Y ou're not going," Kahji said.

"You heard Zanzor." They had consulted with him when they'd realized the papers they'd gathered were legal documents. Not that Zanzor was an expert in mortal legal matters, but he did know more about the mortal realm than most of them, having spent every vacation there for hundreds of years. "It's a summons to court."

"What do we care about mortal courts? We're the Fae. We do not bow to mortal demands. You're *not* going."

Astra dragged in a deep breath and struggled for patience. "But this is a perfect way to gain a broader audience."

"What are you talking about? We don't need an

audience, let alone a broader one."

"Of course, we do. We need the mortals not associated with the government to want us here. We need the mortal residents of Lawrence to want us here."

"Yeah, that's not going to happen. We've *destroyed* their town. Their ridiculous stadium is gone. We took over a large portion of their college campus and half the students fled the area. Fae magic has wreaked havoc on the foundations of their homes and many are in danger of losing their jobs now that you've enclosed the city and they can't get to work."

Astra waved a hand. "Minor details."

"Minor—Astra! Listen to yourself. I know you're a Fae princess, but you can't possibly be that oblivious to the hardships we're causing the mortals here."

Astra groaned.

"You should just tell him, Astra," Andri said.

Kahji's eyes narrowed. "Tell me what? You're a member of the Royal Guard, Andri. And I'm the Captain of that Guard. If you know something, you need to speak up now."

Andri just shook her head. "I'm sorry, sir, but Astra outranks you. She is a princess and I cannot share what she has forbidden."

"Stop glaring at her," Astra snapped. "It's not her fault. We've been helping in the city the last two weeks."

"Helping how?"

"Providing food, fixing crumbling foundations, building a new stadium."

"Building a new—what?"

Astra shrugged. "I figured it would go a long way toward appeasing the mortals, you know, if we built them a new stadium. It's much better than the original. We created it from mostly organic materials and it's quite large. They should be thrilled."

"Should be? Are you telling me you're building a massive structure somewhere in Lawrence without the approval of city officials?"

"How did that even go unnoticed?" Zanzor asked.

"Magic," Astra and Andri chorused.

"Who else have you roped into this and how have I not noticed you've been leaving the shielded areas?" Kahji demanded.

Astra shrugged. "Most of the Guardians of the Veil have been happy to help. It's been rather boring around here since we finished building the stables and the gardens and the castle and well, everything else. The only thing interesting that happens anymore is when the alphabet soup mortals show up."

"Alphabet soup?" Zanzor asked.

"A mortal phrase. I quite like it. Anyway, I'm certain showing up in court in—what was it again? Two weeks' time—will liven things up."

"You're not going and that's final."

wo weeks later

It was madness at the courthouse. Somehow word had spread that the Fae would be in court that day and there were cameras, tourists, journalists, protestors and more all gathered outside.

Two would-be assassins were delivered Fae justice within five minutes of Astra and her Guard arriving on the court steps. A third and fourth assassin were dealt within *inside* the courthouse.

These humans aren't very smart, are they? a haughty voice demanded from below.

Astra glanced down and smiled. "Well, look at you." She crouched down and stroked a hand down the back of the small animal sitting there. "You're so soft. I've never had the opportunity to meet a mortal four-legged being before."

The animal placed her two front paws on Astra's knee and said, *You can pick me up if you like.*

"Why, thank you." Astra swept the animal into her arms and stood, cuddling her against her chest. "What are you doing here anyway?"

Came to see what all the fuss was about, that's all.

"Hey! No cats allowed." A burly security guard barreled toward them. "Put it outside."

Kahji stepped in front of Astra and rested his hand on the hilt of his sword, the same sword he'd already drawn on several humans that morning. "Step away from the Princess."

The guard skidded to a halt, blinked, then blustered, "Look. No animals are allowed inside the courthouse. It's a rule."

"Well, I don't see any purpose to that rule," Astra said. "We'll be breaking it. Come along now." She turned and strode down the hallway.

Her Guard all scrambled to keep up.

Alarms went off as they walked through devices Astra recognized as metal detectors and she smirked a little as the mortal guards scrambled after them, yipping, "No weapons allowed in the courthouse!"

"Do you know where we're going, Astra?" Kahji demanded as he scared the security guards off with a lethal look.

"Not a clue!" Astra said cheerfully. "Let's explore, shall we?"

Kahji groaned as the rest of the Guard chuckled.

It really was the best morning ever.

Astra got to pop her head into courtrooms and see live court in action.

Of course, the mortals weren't too thrilled when she flung open doors and interrupted their proceedings, but Astra found it all utterly fascinating.

Eventually, a couple mortals gathered the courage to approach and instruct them on where to go and they arrived at the correct courtroom.

Astra wasn't as amused once they were inside.

The mortals *still* hadn't learned that their laws did not apply to the Fae.

They tried to show land documents proving they owned the lands where the Fae had now settled—as if the Fae cared what some mortal documents said.

Astra took great delight in educating the mortals, including sharing the fact that land was a living entity that supported all life living upon it, and as such, could not be *owned*. "It would be like you mortals treating your mother or father as a possession," she explained. "They support you, nourish you and you repay them by claiming ownership of them? That's not right. The land *belongs* to no one, but it is mother and father to *everyone*. In fact, it is parent to this cat as much as it is parent to you or me."

The mortals, of course, had many arguments, but it was the woman the others called Your Honor who summarized it all as, "Opinion is not fact, nor is it a legal defense."

Whatever that meant.

Astra heaved a giant sigh. "Fine then. To speak only facts, in our legal defense, the Fae *do* have the right to lay claim to the entirety of the land the university lies upon."

"Excuse me?" The judge looked stunned.

"In fact, the Fae were the original inhabitants of all the land masses of this world. That we retreated from the earth four millennia ago does not change anything."

"If you have no proof—" Your Honor said.

"Proof that four thousand years ago, we Fae owned this land? Since ownership of land is not something we Fae believe in, we do not."

"Well, then—"

"However, we do not require proof."

"Excuse me?"

"We came here today for two reasons and neither is to provide proof to a mortal court we do not answer to. Instead, we are here out of both courtesy and curiosity. It should concern you, though, to know that we are no longer curious, for when the Fae have no curiosity, impatience seeps in, and with impatience comes intolerance, and with intolerance, often, death."

"Are you seriously standing here in *my* courtroom, threatening me?" Your Honor demanded.

"Not at all. I am standing here in a courtroom that exists on top of *Fae* land, and I am making you, and all mortals, a promise. Do *not* make me keep that promise."

Dead silence.

"Let me repeat what is clearly a difficult concept for

you mortals to grasp: *all land in this world was originally inhabited by the immortal Fae.* As such, it has been, currently is and always will be under our protection. Let me repeat that: this land is under *our* protection and we *will* defend it against *any* who would harm it. It is to your great advantage that we have only reclaimed a tiny percentage of the land we protect.

"When we yielded this land to mortals four millennia ago, we did so to the indigenous peoples of this world. The descendants of *those* peoples are the only ones who *may* have equal rights to the lands of this world, and by equal rights, I mean the right to protect the lands, not own them. Unfortunately, since approximately ninety percent of those indigenous peoples were eradicated as part of your nation's historical legacy, this means *very few* mortals have *any* rights to these lands.

"Having said all of that, we are *not* forcing any mortals to leave this city. They may remain and enjoy all the benefits that come from living in a city now controlled by the Fae. We can be quite generous. I hope many will choose to stay and enjoy our hospitality. Good day."

With that, Astra scooped up the cat currently sprawled across the table in front of her and swept from the courtroom, her Guard falling in step behind her.

About time, the cat muttered.

CHAPTER 5

*E*very time Kahji witnessed Astra in full-on Princess of the Universe mode, he got hard.

He found her sexy when she was just breathing, let alone when she brought out the attitude.

The minute she started speaking in that superior, implacable tone—the one that said she'd as soon set the mortals on fire as speak with them—he could barely breathe through the heat that poured through him.

By the fates, he'd been both blessed and cursed to have such a mate.

Though she had finally started speaking to him again after three days of pure torture, things were not good between them.

Anytime he tried to approach the subject of their mating, she simply stood and walked out. He'd finally come to realize how deeply he'd hurt her and how much damage he had done to their matebond.

He couldn't even explain why he'd made that decision so long ago.

It seemed as if he'd waited forever to make her his and he'd looked forward to her hundredth birthday the way a Sorenalaya craved the souls of mortals.

However, the closer that day had come, the more he'd realized she needed more time. More time to grow into her power and into her independence. He could not take from her the destiny she'd been born to, the Fae she would righteously become if allowed to fully mature on her own.

And so he'd done the hardest thing he could ever imagine.

He'd given her another hundred years.

Surely, that would be enough time so that when he did claim her, she would not become lost in *them*, but would remain the strong Princess Astra he knew she would one day become.

And so another hundred years had passed, a thing of torture unlike anything he'd ever experienced. The closer they came to the end of that second century, the lighter he'd felt. He was certain he'd made the right decision and knew that Astra would forgive him for making her wait another hundred years.

Then, something had happened that last year and

his thinking had gotten all twisted again. He'd been sure, absolutely positive, that she still wasn't ready and releasing the pathway was the wrong decision, so he'd held off again.

For another hundred years, he'd thought, but then that birthday came and went and still he never released the path.

As time passed, he became more convinced, rather than less, that it was the right thing to do because he was not the right one for her. It also became easier to hold the pathway closed, to the point that it became instinct and habit rather than conscious thought.

Now, trapped in the mortal realm, far from the Palace of Faerie, he was seeing those eleven hundred years with far greater clarity than ever before, and was wondering how he could have ever thought giving up his mate was the right thing to do. In fact, the more time that passed, the more convinced he became that something was not right about the way he'd continually avoided the bond.

Every hundred years, on the anniversary of Astra's birth, he'd planned to tell her, to release the path, yet every time, he'd chosen not to, and he simply could not understand why.

Of course, he was unworthy of her.

Any Fae would be as Astra was extraordinary, and *no* Fae warrior was worthy of a matebond.

They *all* had blood on their hands while a matebond was a thing of beauty and purity and light.

That was still no reason to deny it, though, especially when it meant dooming Astra to the silence of a life without it.

He had done that to her. *He* had denied her centuries of bonding with her mate, of feeling complete and whole and cherished.

Realizing exactly what he had done, he had no idea how to approach her now, what to say.

He couldn't tell her what he suspected. It didn't make any sense and besides, he couldn't prove any of it, given they were locked out of Faerie.

Worse, it would look like he was trying to pass the responsibility to someone else when the only one to blame for their lack of a matebond was him.

"Are you really going to bring the cat with us?" Dyranel asked.

"Don't be ridiculous," Kahji said at the same time that Astra said, "Of course, I am."

"What?" Kahji exclaimed. "But it's a mortal cat."

"What's your point?"

Kahji had many points, the first being that mortal cats did not belong with Fae creatures who lived for tens of thousands of years. It was never a good idea for a Fae to become attached to any creature whose lifespan was so different from their own.

Unfortunately, he could tell by the look on Astra's face that nothing he said would convince her to leave the cat behind, and might in fact, anger her further, a possibility that made him shudder.

"I was just surprised," he said. "Do you want me to hold her while you mount your—" He broke off as Astra leapt onto her steed, the cat still cradled in her arms. "Never mind then." He swung up on his own horse and with Astra at his side, rode back toward their territory. Or more accurately, *through* their territory toward their more secured territory.

At this point, he imagined it was all pretty secure, especially now that the magic of Faerie had sought out and pulverized all non-Fae weapons within the city, a fact he'd discovered when the first would-be assassin attacked with something the mortals called a baseball bat. Apparently, it was something used in one of their weird battle-games and wasn't considered a weapon at all.

Astra had muttered her new mortal word of the day, "Bullshit," when she'd heard that one.

Kahji grinned at the memory.

"What's so funny?" Astra asked.

It was the first time she'd initiated a conversation in weeks.

"Just remembering the fun we had disarming the mortal assassins."

Astra rolled her eyes. "Like they were a challenge at all."

"You never know. That sculpture looked sharp. It could have done some damage."

"Right."

Kahji chuckled. "So what's up with the cat?"

"Her name's Safira."

"You've already named it?"

"What? Of course not. I would never change someone's name. That would be rude. She told me her name."

"The mortal cat told you its name," Kahji repeated. She couldn't be serious.

"She did, yes."

"You do know that mortal cats cannot speak."

"How would you know?"

"Because it may have been a while since I've traveled to the mortal realm, but I *do* remember that none of the mortal animals were ever capable of speaking."

"Maybe they just didn't like you."

Kahji let out a growl of frustration. "I'm serious, Astra. Mortal cats cannot communicate."

He's not very smart, is he?

Kahji almost fell off his horse, he was so surprised. "Did the cat just talk?" He demanded suspiciously.

"Of course, she did."

"How long have cats been able to talk in this realm?"

"How would I know? Probably forever."

Yes, the cat agreed. *Forever. But only recently have humans been able to understand us.*

"Recently?" Kahji repeated. "As in the current generation has evolved the ability to understand animals?"

No. Recently as in the last couple of weeks. None of the humans could understand me, and then, suddenly, some of them could.

Though you're the first ones who have responded.

All the others have just stared wide-eyed, then exclaimed they were going mad and ran away. Though a few called me demon cat first.

"I'm speechless," Kahji said.

"Well, that's a first," Astra said.

"Not really. I have no idea what to say to you to make things right, how to apologize, how to explain."

"Then don't."

Oooh. What did he do? Safira peered around Astra's shoulder at Kahji.

Suddenly realizing that Astra couldn't just walk out of the room—though she might decide to ride away—Kahji decided to plead his case, even though it meant the other Guardians might hear him grovel.

"He broke my heart," Astra said to the cat.

I don't think that's something he can make right. Is it?

"No. It is not."

Nevertheless. "Astra, I have adored you from the moment I met you."

"Please don't."

"If you think I kept this from you because I don't want you, nothing could be further from the truth."

"Kahji, please."

Kahji guided his horse in front of hers, then circled around as her mount came to a stop. He angled close and cradled her face in his hands, lifting her chin and catching her gaze with his.

The rest of the Guard circled around them, facing outward, providing a shield from the many mortals gathered around, watching as they progressed down what was left of Eleventh Street.

"You have always been the reason for every breath in my body, the life in my limbs, the hope in my heart."

"Kahji."

"I will spend the rest of my days regretting my idiocy and striving to show you how very much I adore you. If you choose never to accept me as your mate, I will understand, but I will never stop trying to prove my love for you."

*A*stra's breath hitched in her throat as she stared into Kahji's eyes.

She wanted to believe him, but a part of her was still terrified he would change his mind.

"You spent eleven hundred years walking away, Kahji. Why should I believe you want me now?"

"I have always wanted you, Astra. Always. I cannot explain what happened or why I became so convinced that I was not the right mate for you, but I am here now and I promise, on my honor, that I will never walk away again."

"If you feel this way, then why is our pathway still closed?"

"That is not a step I will take without your permission, Astra. I held it closed, without consulting you, for over a thousand years. I will not open it again without your consent."

The need for him was an ache inside her heart, a yearning from the depths of her being, to hear his voice inside her head, to feel the forging of their path.

She could not deny either one of them the matebond they had both yearned a thousand years for.

"Open the path, Kahji."

He stared into her eyes for a moment, searching for something, perhaps proof of her sincerity. "Very well, my love."

Something deep inside pulled tight, then released with a snap.

Astra?

Kahji.

"Kahji, Princess Astra, I am sorry to interrupt," Rashideh said, "but the mortals are becoming entirely too bold. We need to keep moving."

Astra giggled. "Yes. This is not the right time or place." *Come, Kahji. Let us go home. Well, to our temporary home, anyway. We have a mating ceremony and celebration to plan.*

The incandescent joy on Kahji's face stole all the breath from Astra's lungs.

They rode the rest of the way in silence, but it was not an empty one. It was filled with things unsaid, the pathway connecting the two of them vibrating with love and joy, and the feel of their matebond waiting, poised on the precipice of destiny.

CHAPTER 6

"The mortals are following us," Zanzor reported a few moments later.

"Interesting, isn't it?" Astra said. "The magic of Faerie is transforming everything. The lands, the animals, even the people."

"What are you talking about?" Kahji asked.

"The mortals must have sensed that something momentous is about to happen and that's why they're following us."

"Or maybe they're just interested in the Fae."

Astra grinned. "Perhaps. Either way, we should let them attend our matebond ceremony. They can serve as witnesses to the joy of a Fae mating. Perhaps it will soften their hearts toward us."

"I wouldn't count on it," Kahji said, "and they can be witnesses from behind the shield."

"Then let's have our ceremony near the lake. It's close enough to the shield, they'll be able to get a good view."

"Whatever you want, my love."

Two hours later, Astra stood facing Kahji, next to the lake she had claimed in a territory expansion several weeks before, with her heart in her throat.

The Guardians were all there as witnesses, as were a large number of mortals on the other side of the shield.

Even Safira was there, standing on a bench, watching.

"Astra." Kahji drew in a deep breath, then spoke the traditional vows solemnly. "I see eternity in your eyes and no matter the length of our days, I shall know peace so long as you are by my side. I offer you everything that I am, everything that I have been and everything I've yet to become, in this realm and in any other, in this lifetime and in all the rest."

Astra smiled, for that bit about realms was his own addition.

"With you, *for* you, Astra, I am my best self."

The joy Astra felt, listening to Kahji speak vows she'd begun to believe she would never hear, was incandescent, as was the joy she felt in speaking those same vows back to *him,* the one Fae she had loved from the beginning and would love through all the remaining days of her life.

"Kahji. I see eternity in your eyes and no matter the length of our days, I shall know peace so long as you are by my side. I offer you everything that I am, everything that I have been and everything I've yet to become, in this realm and in any other, in this lifetime and in all the rest."

Kahji grinned at her and she finished her vows with a smile on her face. "With you, *for* you, I am my best self."

A thousand blessings be upon this mating. It was the cat, Safira, who spoke the traditional Fae blessing, but it was Queen Naira's voice and Queen Naira's magic that rained down upon Astra and Kahji in tiny little bursts of power, a royal blessing from the Fae side of the Veil, bringing their matebond to throbbing life.

Before Kahji had a chance to even think of kissing his mate, the other Guardians had leapt forward and separated the two.

In Faerie, the Fae would travel for days to attend a Fae mating celebration, for they were traditionally full of laughter, music and dancing, and were an opportunity to celebrate the joining of two Fae souls.

Though no Fae traveled to attend Kahji's mating celebration with Astra, and though the number of Fae in attendance was possibly the lowest number in the history of the Fae—six Royal Guardians and thirteen Guardians of the Veil—the celebration was still as joyful and as full of tradition as Kahji could have hoped for.

The Fae Guardians outdid themselves.

They used earth magic to coax the land into providing a dance floor and the trees and wind into providing music.

They whirled Astra and Kahji onto the dance floor and worked hard to keep the two close enough to yearn for each other, but not close enough to actually touch.

The mortals on the other side of the shield leapt into their own preparations. They set up their own dance floor, brought out musical instruments and joined the celebration.

The mortal crowd grew as word spread that a Fae celebration was happening.

Children arrived and ran around, laughing and dancing, and though there was a shield between Fae and mortal, it felt like one big celebration.

"You were right," Kahji called to Astra as several

Guardians whirled her past where he was dancing with Dyranel and Zanzor.

"About what?" she called to him over Talveney's shoulder.

Kahji had to wait to answer because Dyranel pulled him into an intricate dance step that required all his concentration and when he looked up, Astra had disappeared behind a wall of Guardians.

It was a while before Kahji saw her again. This time, she was in Rashideh's arms."About inviting the mortals. It feels like a true mating celebration."

"That's because it is one!" Rashideh exclaimed as he whirled Astra into Kahji's arms.

Not one to miss an opportunity like that, Kahji immediately pulled Astra close and kissed her.

*A*stra had waited over a thousand years for this one kiss, but as heat rolled through her, she knew she would have waited ten thousand more.

She lifted high onto her toes, wrapped her arms around Kahji's shoulders and strained closer, pouring everything she had into that kiss.

Breathing him in—*her mate, her fated one, her life*—Astra lost all sense of time and place.

"I do believe that's quite enough of that." Toren pulled her from Kahji and though she strained to get back to him, the Guardians formed a wall between her and Kahji again, and Toren whirled her into Lumina's arms.

She giggled as Lumina swept her around in a circle, then sent her spinning into Andri's arms, who spun her into Korel's.

In this way, the Guardians kept her and Kahji dancing far from each other most of the night, though every once in a while, they conspired for them to meet on the dance floor.

Sometimes, it was barely long enough for them to touch a hand. Other times, they had just enough time for a flaming hot kiss before they were separated again.

As the hours passed, the heat between them built until Astra could barely breathe for wanting her mate, especially since Kahji kept talking to her through their bond, murmuring delicious things to her, even as they were kept apart.

Though they were now mated, their matebond secure, he was still courting her, wooing her, seducing her with his voice.

I cannot wait to taste you again, my sweet Astra.

I've waited centuries for our mating, and tonight, when we lie skin to skin, I will remember those many lonely years and take my time making you mine.

Astra, my love, you are a fire in my blood and I burn for you.

Every moment we are together for the rest of our lives will be a blessing I will never take for granted.

I look forward to peeling that gown from your body and learning every contour of it with my hands and my tongue.

Ah, my love, my Fae princess, my Astra, I wonder how you will taste.

Sweet and exquisitely fine, no doubt.

It was only as the skies around them lightened, heralding the approaching dawn, that Astra and Kahji were finally allowed to escape to have their own, more private celebration.

By that time, Astra was as close to spontaneously combusting as she imagined any Fae had ever been.

Holding hands, she and Kahji ran around the pond and headed for the castle, the cat, Safira, who had joined in the dancing, at times weaving between dancers' feet and at others cradled in Fae arms, darting behind them.

Kahji led Astra through the front entrance of the castle and veered them immediately to the left.

Astra had expected him to take her up the back stairs to where the bedrooms were.

Instead, he let her toward the western tower.

Astra, Lumina and Andri had spent hours pouring over images of mortal castles, particularly the towers, and had used air and earth magic to perfect their versions of them.

They had tunneled out a ramp inside the towers that wound round and round to the roof. The earth and vines closed off the top of the ramp in poor weather, but otherwise, it led right out onto the roof of the tower.

They had also created a walkway that ran across the front wall of the castle, connecting the two towers.

Astra found the shape of the battlements at the top of the walls of the towers and the walkway to be charming and preferred not to think of how mortals had used them to wage war.

Though it had taken quite some time to create the towers and walkway, they really were just decorative in nature. The Guardians sometimes used them to see far into the distance, to judge where mortals were in relation to the shield that surrounded them, but otherwise, they weren't exactly the heart of the castle.

As such, Astra wondered what Kahji was planning, leading her up the ramp. Perhaps he intended for them to watch the sun rise up there. It would undoubtedly provide an amazing view.

The lighting in the tower changed as the artificial light from the lanterns hung along the walls gave way to the natural light of the dawning day as they reached the end of the ramp and arrived on the roof of the tower.

When she saw what awaited them there, Astra gasped. "How is this possible? We didn't even know we were going to have our ceremony today until just this afternoon."

"The Guardians have been slipping away in groups of two and three to work on this throughout the celebration."

"That's so sweet. It's incredible." The entire area had been transformed into the most beautiful of rooftop gardens. There was a pathway that stretched around the edge of the tower, but the rest of the roof was entirely abloom and at the center of that fragrant, extraordinary garden, a bed created of leaves, flowering vines and juniper branches awaited them.

"The Guardians tell me they learned their lesson when building Kalina and Thorne's bed, which is why they didn't try to elevate ours." Kahji chuckled.

Astra had no idea why that was so amusing, but she wasn't really interested in hearing the story, at least not at that moment. *What do you say we test out their creation?*

Kahji grinned. *I think that is a splendid idea.*

Race you there! She ran down the path leading to the bed with Kahji just one step behind her.

When she was mere feet from her goal, he hooked an arm around her waist and spun her toward him.

He launched them at the bed, turning so that he hit first and she landed on top of him.

Kahji.

Astra, my love.

They rolled across the bed, kissing and straining to get closer.

Kahji surged back, dragged his tunic over his head, then fell down to kiss Astra once more.

Another few moments of endless, drugging kisses, then he wrestled her gown from her before setting down again to stroke and kiss her and learn what made her burn.

A third time he left her, this time to wrestle with the rest of his clothing.

Astra stripped her undergarments away and lay back to stare at her mate as he kicked off his boots and dragged his trousers free.

She barely had time to admire his gorgeous, muscular form before he was settling back over her, kissing her thoroughly.

Then, there were no more thoughts at all as he clasped her hands in his, stared into her eyes and sank deep.

Kahji. She gasped for breath and lunged upward, burying her face in his neck and wrapping her legs around him.

By the fates, you make me burn. The raspy rumble of his voice made her shudder and a deep fluttering began.

Ah, my love. Kahji settled even more heavily over her, holding himself still, making her writhe in an agony of need.

Kahji, please!

Finally, *finally*, he began to move, pulling out and then surging forward again and again, causing her to cry out as the friction and heat rose to an unbearable degree.

She flung her head back and stared at the skies above them, eyes going blind to the streaks of orange and red setting the world afire as she burned below them in a conflagration of heat, desire and breathless ecstasy.

K ahji's heart pounded as he lay sprawled upon the bed his fellow Guardians had built for him and his princess mate. With Astra sprawled at his side, her head pillowed on his chest, his fingers gently toying with her blue curls, he wondered how the fates had ever deemed him worthy of this incredible gift.

He felt so wonderfully blessed, so fortunate to be

the mate of this singular, extraordinary Fae, he knew he would never be able to express to her how much she truly meant to him and how grateful he was that she had forgiven him his centuries-long mistake.

"Astra, my love," he murmured as she traced her fingers across his Guardian markings.

They had begun as just a few tiny, black leaves stretching up the left side of his neck, but over the centuries had expanded outward, a trailing black vine that stretched across his left shoulder and down his arm, wrapping it in an intricate sleeve of vines.

More recently, the vine on his neck had sprouted new leaves that trailed down the left side of his body, bypassing his groin area to wrap around his thigh.

He often wondered how far the vines would travel, whether they would eventually cross to the right side of his body or if this was as far as they would go.

The markings were part of him, even as they grew and expanded, and he rarely thought about them anymore, other than to note when a new vine sprouted somewhere.

Today, however, he adored them because Astra was slowly stroking her fingers across his chest, tracing the vines' paths down, then up again, spreading heat everywhere she touched.

You know, that's going to get you—oomph. Something landed on his stomach with enough force to expel all his breath and distract him from what he'd been saying. *What the—* he lifted his head, then rolled his eyes at the sight of the cat sitting on his stomach, glaring at him.

Did you really have to bring the cat?

Astra giggled.

The cat's presence was annoying, but it did remind Kahji of something he'd meant to ask. "Did I just imagine Queen Naira's voice blessing our union?"

"I don't think so. After all, my mother is quite powerful. Still, even I was surprised to realize she'd managed to reach through the Veil to bless us on our mating day."

"You'd think she could have found a better candidate for delivering her message than a mortal cat."

Safira hissed and swiped out at him, drawing blood.

"Ow, you little beast!"

"You insulted her. What do you expect?"

"I bet the cat doesn't talk at all. It was probably just your mother messing with us."

Astra lifted up and gave him an incredulous look. "Do you really believe my mother, the Queen of Faerie, used her magic to break through the barrier and reach out to her daughter who is trapped on the mortal side of the realm, just so that she could 'mess with me?'"

"Well, when you put it like that," Kahji grumbled.

I stand by my original observation, Safira said. *The male of the species, any species, just isn't that smart.*

Astra grinned. "We probably shouldn't say that out loud, Safira. At least not where the males can hear us."

Just making sure he understands his place. Beneath me. And you, of course. Well, and every other female on the planet.

Kahji let out a snort of disgust and Astra giggled again.

"I see how this is going to go. Ganged up on by a couple females." Kahji surged upward, causing Safira to launch away with a soft hiss, then turned and bore Astra to the bed, settling heavily over her once more. "I don't mind though." He captured her lips in a searing kiss, murmuring against them as he sank deep, "You can gang up on me anytime you like."

CHAPTER 7

The following days were amazing.

When the sun rose in the sky, the garden around them rose to shield them from the worst of its effects, forming a canopy over their mating bed, then retracted as the sun fell so that they could make love under the stars.

Each morning, they walked across the walkway to the eastern tower where they found a table set up with food and drinks, a new feast provided every morning by the Guardians.

And so the first week of their mating passed, with delicious food and endless lovemaking.

When they finally emerged from the tower, they were greeted with cheers and congratulations.

"Princess Astra, Captain." Dyranel stepped

forward. "Much has happened over the past seven days. Fae have begun arriving in the city of Lawrence from all over the Americas, from wherever they were traveling when the crossings closed. There are encampments as far west as Topeka, as far east as Kansas City, as far south as Wichita and as far north as Omaha.

"The secondary shield around Lawrence is intact. It has not expanded. However, the magic has traveled well beyond our borders and a third shield has gone up around the larger territory."

Astra had to be misunderstanding. "A shield went up without us actively putting it in place? None of you made it happen?"

The Guardians shook their heads.

"What about the other Fae? Could one of them have replicated her shield?" Kahji asked.

"Several of us have been traveling out to make contact with the Fae and to gain an understanding of this third shield," Yiveren, one of the Guardians of the Veil, said. "It truly is a construct of Faerie, made purely of its magic."

"He's right," Toren said. "Astra's shields are a combination of her magic and that of Faerie itself. This third shield has nothing of the Fae, but is everything of Faerie."

"We believe it went up to provide protection to the

Fae who have not made it inside the secondary shield yet," Dyranel said.

"Unfortunately, the mortals are now looking at us as an aggressive and hostile force, here to overthrow their government and destroy their world," Zanzor said. "They have attempted multiple attacks, but the magic of Faerie defends itself quite aggressively. Every mortal weapon within the shield or a hundred miles outside it has been destroyed and no mortal with aggressive intentions has been allowed to cross any of the shields.

"Of course, that hasn't helped with those aggressors already inside them. There have been reports of Fae deaths, though none have gone unpunished. Either the Fae themselves have executed the aggressors or the magic of Faerie has literally incinerated them. This has caused a bit of a panic among the mortals and there was a surge in aggression approximately two days ago."

"You should have come to us immediately," Kahji said with a scowl.

"With all due respect, Captain, there was nothing you could have done," Dyranel said. "None of us can control the magic of Faerie. It wants what it wants."

Astra shivered to hear those words she had often used when describing her own magic.

It wants what it wants.

"The magic of Faerie has made its stance quite clear," Dyranel continued. "It is claiming land for the

Fae who are trapped here and it is defending those Fae quite viciously."

"The interesting thing," Zanzor said, "is that not all the mortals hate what is happening. Many have traveled here to join what they are calling the miracle revolution."

"Miracle revolution? What do they mean by that?" Kahji demanded.

"I believe it refers to the miracle many mortals have hoped for when it comes to the health of their planet," Dyranel said. "They believe this is the revolution needed for the earth to heal itself from all the damage the mortals themselves have caused."

"You should also know that the primary shield isn't holding every mortal out anymore," Zanzor said.

"What do you mean?" Astra exclaimed.

"The mortals are getting inside our primary shield?" Kahji repeated incredulously.

"They are," Zanzor said. "It appears they are all of indigenous blood and they have come to align them-selves with the Fae and to express their gratitude and hope for a healthier world."

"All of this happened in just seven days?" Astra exclaimed.

"A video of your mating celebration went viral," Dyranel said.

"What is viral?" Kahji asked.

"A mortal recorded the mating celebration and posted it on a bunch of internet social sites," Dyranel explained. "It was shared over and over again, until it went this thing called viral. It even eventually made its way onto the Fae web. Our brethren saw the mating celebration and they all celebrated with us wherever they were."

"It's really quite amazing," Zanzor said. "We thought your mating celebration was only attended by nineteen Fae, but instead, hundreds celebrated with us throughout the Americas."

"Yes, and when the celebration was over, they started traveling here," Dyranel said, "many of them undertaking an extraordinarily long journey."

"One couple I spoke with came from as far south as Patagonia," Zanzor said.

"How have they been managing it?" Astra asked.

"Horses, mortal transportation such as trains and buses and a whole lot of magic, especially when crossing borders."

The concept of borders was so strange to Astra. To require documents to travel from one place to the next seemed barbaric. All Fae were a community of one, welcome anywhere in Faerie at any time.

Not that they hadn't waged wars throughout their history. It was perhaps the one great tragedy of being such a long-lived race of beings. After so many centuries of living, it could become difficult to find hope in the future, especially if a Fae never found his or her mate.

When that happened, Fae mostly Faded from the world, becoming Sorenalaya, a weaker, more insubstantial version of their most beastly selves. Thin to the point of transparency, armed with claws and fangs, the Sorenalaya craved human flesh and souls and hunted along the borderlands between Faerie and the mortal world, hoping to cross over and feast.

The Guardians were tasked with ending their pain and suffering and sending them into the light. It darkened a Guardian's soul, but also made the Guardians a bright, shining light for all the Fae, for they were the most honorable of them all.

Skirmishes with the Sorenalaya, though, were not wars.

Wars came when something far worse than the Sorenalaya was born of a Fae's darkness, when the Fae who should have Faded remained part of the world instead and were consumed by their darkness, spreading it to those around them.

This was when war happened, when the Fae had to rise up against one of their own and fight the armies of the dark, to bring light back to the world.

There had only ever been one war in Astra's lifetime and she had been a little girl at the time. It had taken six hundred thousand Fae and sixty years to bring that dark Fae down.

Astra hoped never to see the likes of her again.

"My love, are you okay?" Kahji cupped her cheek in concern.

Astra shook away her memories of the dark. "Sorry. Just a ghost walking over my grave."

"What a horrible mortal phrase," Zanzor said, giving an exaggerated shudder.

Horrible, perhaps, but that doesn't make it any less accurate. Safira wound around Astra's legs, rubbing against them. *Do not allow the ghosts of the past to distract you from what is happening right now, Princess Astra.*

"Yes, you're right," Astra murmured. "What should we do?"

Zanzor dragged in a deep breath. "You're not going to like this, Kahji."

Kahji scowled. "What are you thinking?"

"The Fae need to see their Princess, but they also need to see the two of you together. They need to know that there is hope and that the Throne continues to thrive, even here in the mortal realm, so far from home. More, the mortals who would be our allies need to see the two of you together, your strength and your bond. We need to make our own viral video."

Astra giggled. "I don't think we can guarantee a

video will go viral, Zanzor. It simply happens or it doesn't."

He just stared at her.

She rolled her eyes. "Fine. I suppose we could use our glamour and embed some magic in the video and compel them to watch it, but I'm not sure compelling the mortals is a good idea."

Kahji chuckled.

"What?"

"That you believe they will need to be compelled to watch any video starring you, the Fae Princess Astra, is ridiculous, but Zanzor is right. I do not like this plan."

"We're already exposed, Kahji. There is no containing this situation. The only thing we can do is move forward and I absolutely agree that our Fae citizens need to see us and know that we are here for them, that we are working hard to find them a way home. It only makes sense to allow the mortals to see us at the same time. So as a famous mortal captain once said, let's make it so."

K ahji hated this plan with a passion, though he wasn't exactly sure why, other than that he wanted to protect his mate and this plan felt reckless.

Astra reassured him multiple times that she could take care of herself, that no mortal could possibly harm her, to which he reminded her that many Fae had already fallen.

They had a list of the Fae taken from them too soon: seventeen names that they knew of, so far, and all of them knew there could be more.

At highest risk were those solitary Fae who had been traveling alone with no warriors to defend them and no glamour to shield them from human eyes during those six long moments when the Veils had fallen and the magic of Faerie had become inaccessible.

The bad news was that none of them knew how many Fae were out there. They had an estimate only.

The Guardians of the Veil monitored all crossings and therefore, believed they had a general idea of how many Fae were typically on the mortal side of the Veils at any given time.

Their best estimate was approximately five thousand.

Still, it was an estimate only and they warned it could be off by a significant amount.

Kahji hated that his mate felt responsible for every single one of those Fae, that she felt compelled to find them and protect them.

All he cared about was protecting her, but the reality was, though she insisted she never wanted the throne of Faerie, to all those Fae currently trapped in the Americas, she *was* the throne.

They looked to her for answers and for hope.

All Kahji could do was stand at her side and support her as she stepped further into her destiny as a Royal Princess of the Fae.

They had been traveling for weeks now, slowly exploring the territories Faerie had claimed for the Fae, interacting with the inhabitants of those territories, both Fae and mortal alike.

Though Astra knew Kahji didn't like it, she appreciated that he never once protested when she hugged Fae who looked lost, when she swept small Fae children up into her arms and entertained them with a bit of Fae magic, or when she held one Fae as she wept for her orphaned children in Faerie while her mate looked helplessly on.

The days were difficult to endure, hearing so many Fae stories of who had been left behind, of why the Fae had come to the mortal realm in the first place—to shop or travel or enjoy a night out with friends—most of the reasons so frivolous, the Fae were leveled by the consequence of such a seemingly innocent decision.

Not worth it, was the cry Astra heard over and over again.

What the Fae had gained in their travels to the mortal realm wasn't worth the terrible sacrifice now being asked of them.

After long days spent with the Fae, Astra and her Guard passed their evenings with the indigenous communities who had traveled from around Kansas and beyond to meet the Fae.

The various tribes shared their traditional stories of how land and lives had been lost in the distant past. Despite the passage of generations and the distance that had been gained from those terrible times, if not from their consequences, the tragedy of it all broke Astra's heart.

That mortals had not cherished each life as part of their community of one, that they had not seen the land as a nourishing parent to be shared by all, that they had instead bathed those lands in blood, steeping them in violence and tears, made her heart tremble.

The nights she spent in Kahji's arms.

He held her as she wept a storm of tears, purging her sorrow and grief from the stories she'd heard that day, then he loved her tenderly through the night hours, setting her body aflame and healing her anew.

Then every morning, they got up to do it all over again.

"The website we set up is getting two million hits a day," Talveney reported at the end of a long day nearly six weeks later.

"I can't keep up with the comments," Andri complained. "I've tried every bit of spellwork I can think of to purge all the racist and hateful comments, but it just doesn't work. Every spell ends up purging some comments it shouldn't and leaving others that it should. It's driving me mad."

Kahji chuckled. He couldn't believe the conversations they were having anymore—the Fae dealing with technology, managing websites and recording videos. It was enough to make him doubt his own sanity. "Well, better you two than me. I do not understand this mortal technology at all."

"It's not so mortal anymore," Talveney said. "At this point, it's really a construct of Faerie."

"Which is why it makes no sense that the spells won't work," Andri said.

"Maybe because if we purge everything we don't want to hear, all we end up with is an echo chamber,"

Astra said. "Perhaps we need to hear what the hateful ones are saying, just so that we can be sure and address the hate, purge it by refuting their words, rather than scrubbing them out entirely."

"Huh." Andri appeared to think about that for a moment. "That might explain why the spells are scooping up the worst of the offenders, the ones there's no point in engaging, like the death threats and things like that, but leaving the opinions of close-minded idiots. Honestly, I don't have to refute them because others—many, many others—take them on beautifully."

"Well, there you have it," Kahji said. "I say, don't waste your time on those idiots. In fact, it'd be nice if we could stop with the recordings as well."

Astra rolled her eyes at him, making him grin.

Even though he understood their purpose, Kahji hated the videos Talveney and Andri had Astra making.

It was why Kahji had insisted on being at her side in every single video and had then made a point of standing, arms crossed, scowling at the camera the entire time.

Astra found it hilarious.

Talveney and Andri just rolled their eyes at him.

As for Kahji, he simply wanted anyone watching to know viscerally that targeting Astra was to risk the most terrible of Fae executions possible.

He would never admit it, but even he could see the

videos were having positive results as they showcased Astra's work traveling through the territories.

Conversations she had with both Fae and mortals were, with permission, recorded and posted on their website, no explanation given, just a title, something like "Meeting with representatives from The Kaw Nation, People of the Southwind" or "Conversations with Fae working to clean the waters of Kansas."

It was the Fae's hope that over time the videos would help the mortals understand the true nature of the lands that supported them and the inherited role and responsibilities that came with being stewards of the land, whether they be Fae or mortal, indigenous or not.

Still, it was the video of a tiny mortal child running up to Astra, arms high for a hug that had garnered the most views.

Astra's beaming smile as she swept the child into her arms, listened to her babble and cuddled her as she napped on Astra's shoulder was the one video that seemed to have charmed an entire nation.

The hostilities from the mortal government had subsided, mostly because it had become clear there would be no displacing the Fae and that they would meet violence of any sort within their territories with swift, Fae justice.

For the most part, the Fae left the mortal courts to

deal with their mortal criminals, but that did not mean the Fae would not strike back should those criminals target the Fae, including when those criminals were government officials.

The Fae also intervened when they became aware of mortals committing crimes against other mortals.

In fact, criminals were delivered with frequent regularity to the police stations closest to where the Fae were staying.

And so the months had passed, with the center of the country known as the United States of America undergoing an extraordinary transformation as more and more Fae arrived and as the land was healed.

Astra assumed a similar transformation was happening on the eastern seaboard, stretching from Washington, D.C. to New York City, but she couldn't be certain because they still had no news from inside that shield.

The shield that had come down around D.C. in the moments following the Fae's arrival had expanded outward to envelop Baltimore, Philadelphia, New York City and all the territories between. It had then frozen there and nothing had happened since.

Fae had initially gathered along that shield's border as well, but when they weren't admitted and no one came out to greet them, they eventually turned toward

Kansas and the Princess whose mating ceremony they had celebrated from afar.

With their arrival came the return of the majority of the Guardian unit Astra had sent east.

"The shield allowed Mitaru through, then Kalina and Thorne, but it refused the rest of us," Jeniah explained. "We wanted to stay and wait, but Kalina directed us to lead the rest of the Fae here, to see if you had new orders for us. The three of them were going to do their best to track Glory down. Mitaru seemed certain they would find her."

That was the last they'd heard from the east.

No other Guardians they sent were able to penetrate the eastern shield and so Lawrence, Kansas, became the mortal home to the Fae Throne, and the territories surrounding it, home to the Fae themselves.

Astra, though she'd had no desire to become queen, found herself serving in that role to the Fae refugees who arrived seeking hope and a bit of Faerie to comfort them in the darkness.

Astra faced that same darkness and it was Kahji who kept her sane, who kept her hope alive, even when she despaired of ever seeing her sister again, of seeing her brothers, of gaining access to their homelands once more.

Each night, when they retired, wherever they were,

Astra turned to Kahji to keep that darkness at bay and this night was no different.

Leaving Talveney and Andri debating what to title the latest video they had just uploaded, Kahji led Astra up the stairs toward their chambers.

When they arrived, he undressed her gently, caressing and dropping a reverent kiss upon each bit of flesh revealed along the way.

Though he took his time with her, he stripped his own clothes with an economy of movement and gently lowered her to their bed, following her down.

My love, he murmured, linking their hands together, palm to palm, staring into her eyes as he sank deep.

Kahji, she whispered, pulling him close, burying her face in his neck and breathing in his familiar, heady scent. *You are my everything.*

As you are mine. Mate. Beloved. Best friend.

Though uncertainty defined their lives, there were no doubts in these moments, no questions, no worries, no insecurities.

They were simply *one.*

GLORY

CHAPTER 1

MORTAL SIDE OF THE EASTERN VEIL,
WASHINGTON, D.C.

This was the third Ceremony of the Veil that had occurred in Princess Glory's lifetime, but only the second where she'd been called to serve as royal witness. Even so, she knew two things immediately.

One, the Guardians of the Eastern Veil did not hesitate to perform their sacred duty. They poured their life force over the Veil in a breathtaking act of honor and devotion to the Fae.

And two, their sacrifice was failing.

The fractures in the Veil were not disappearing as they should, but instead were multiplying swiftly.

Before Glory could decide on a course of action, the ground trembled, causing the waters around her to ripple and surge outward, almost as if she were standing in the ocean, rather than a mortal-made pool.

A flash of light exploded from the Veil and everything went dark.

Glory woke surrounded by water.

For a split second, she remembered nothing, then it all came back in a rush.

The Reflecting Pool.

The Eastern Veil.

The mortals on every side.

"Princess Glory." Talvenia, the Captain of her Royal Guard, held out a hand—the one not holding her sword—and pulled Glory to her feet. "The Veil is down."

The rest of the Royal Guard stood around them, swords drawn, facing the mortals who gaped in awe, some of them struggling to their feet, others frozen where they had fallen.

Of all the places in the mortal realm where a doorway to Faerie might have stood, this was not the location Glory would have chosen.

Too many mortals.

Too many cameras.

Too many things that could go wrong.

One only had to look toward Faerie to see that truth.

The doorway that led into their realm was no longer shielded by the Eastern Veil. Instead, the lands and skies of Faerie were completely exposed, providing a glimpse into a world few mortals had ever seen.

Worse, the glamour the Fae had projected to shield themselves from mortal eyes was also down. This was clear from the way the mortals stared even as they recorded everything.

This was a disaster.

At that moment, Fae Guardians poured through the doorway.

As they marched past to stand as a physical, living shield between the mortals and the entrance to Faerie, Glory recognized them as those tasked with strengthening the Eastern Veil.

They would have expected to be nothing but dust on the wind by now, their life force given in tribute to strengthen the Veil.

Instead, they were here, still alive, standing on mortal grounds, the final line of defense for Faerie and all of the Fae.

"We should retreat, Princess Glory," Talvenia said. "Leave the Guardians to protect the entrance to Faerie and—" She broke off as the Veil yanked energy from all of the Fae standing there.

"It's too late," Glory gasped, struggling to breathe through the whiplash sensation of her magic being used to reform the Veil before returning to her in a massive rush of power.

Glory swayed in place, staring at the Veil. It was back, but somehow *wrong.* She reached out with her magic, attempting to get a feel for what she was sensing.

"Why is it transparent?" Xilarin asked. "It should be a doorway, not a window."

"The mortals can still *see* Faerie," Raiyana said, glancing around, a worried look on her face.

"At least it's back up," Talvenia said. "It's stable, right?"

"It's stable." Glory shoved her magic harder at the Veil, testing its strength, probing for a way in. "It's also—"

"What?" Xilarin asked.

"Locked."

"Against *us?*" Raiyana demanded.

"Against everyone, I think." Glory splashed through the water toward the Veil. She reached out and ran her hand over it.

Solid.

Fairly vibrating with magic.

And completely sealed shut.

"How is that even possible?" One of the Guardians of the Veil demanded. Glory thought his name was Nako.

Before she could respond—not that she had an explanation to offer—one of the Fae shouted, "Guardians, defend the Princess. Guard the entrance to Faerie!"

"What's happening?" Glory whirled away from the Veil, but all she could see was her Royal Guard, who surrounded her in force.

Shouts and a strange popping sound filled the air.

Something hit Raiyana, spinning her toward Glory, a fine red mist spraying the air. "Princess—" she gasped as her knees buckled.

Glory lunged forward to catch Raiyana as she fell, but something plowed into Glory with the force of ten thousand Sorenalaya and flung her back.

Time seemed to slow as she fell, pain spreading fire to every nerve in her body.

When she hit the water, droplets sprayed upward in a dance so slow, they almost seemed as if they weren't moving at all.

Glory stared at those droplets, even as she sank below the surface, the fire spreading until it reached the core of who she was and touched the wild magic hiding there.

As the water droplets began their inexorable fall back toward earth, that feral, Fae magic that Glory had spent a millennia containing, exploded from every pore of her being and erased the world in a white wave of power.

Mitaru was born to be a Guardian of the Veil.

At the end of his thousand years of service, he'd gifted his life force to the Veil and had stepped into eternity, eyes wide open.

It was a sacrifice he'd been honored to make, but it had not ended as expected.

He should be nothing but memory now, a tiny speck of dust that had burned itself out for the Fae and all of Faerie.

Instead, he was still flesh and bone, living in exile, along with his Guardian unit, on the mortal side of the Veils.

He'd initially believed the Guardians of the Veil were being punished for failing in their sacred duty, but not all Guardians of the Veil had made it to the mortal side. Many were still safe in Faerie while an unknown number of innocent Fae who had been traveling in the mortal realm, were now trapped there.

Two months had passed since the Unveiling of the Fae and the freezing of the Veils and they had no more answers today than when they'd first been exiled.

Mitaru's unit had been stationed that first month at the Western Veil, where Princess Astra had used the magic of Faerie to claim territory in the state of Kansas. By the time Mitaru and his unit left Kansas to travel east, the shield she had constructed around the territory had already expanded several times.

There was no telling how far it had progressed in the weeks since.

The northeastern shield, by contrast, had constructed itself almost immediately after the fall of the Eastern Veil, taking mere moments to claim all of the territories between Washington, D.C. and New York City in a vast display of power.

That shield was now frozen in place, an impenetrable barrier that had not expanded since.

More disturbing was the lack of communication or any sign of life from behind that barrier. No one had been seen emerging from it, nor had anyone been able to cross it. Though both mortals and Fae had gathered along the shield, none could see past it to what was happening inside.

The only clues they had were the videos broadcast live from the National Mall at the moment of the Fae's unveiling, but all connectivity had been lost the moment the shield went up.

Those videos were the only record of what had happened that day at the Eastern Veil and they showed very little.

Guardians pouring through the Eastern Veil, landing in the Lincoln Memorial Reflecting Pool, then surrounding the Veil.

Mortal soldiers running toward them, shouting.

Chaos as mortals screamed and ran.

The horrifying sound of gunfire—a sound Mitaru had never heard before arriving in the mortal world two months before.

A brilliant flash of light that was starting to fade when a secondary explosion of light collided with it.

Then nothing.

The Fae speculated that the shield had formed in the wake of that explosion of light and that perhaps both had been caused by Princess Glory, though few had seen her wield power of that magnitude.

Despite this, rumor had it that Princess Glory's magic was even stronger than Princess Astra's.

Mitaru found that hard to believe, though, especially

after witnessing the pure power of Princess Astra in the aftermath of the Western Veil's fall and the mortals' attack on the Fae.

He was convinced he was right and that Princess Astra had to be the stronger sister when four weeks after the Unveiling, she commanded Mitaru's unit commander and best friend, Kalina, to take half her unit to find and protect Glory.

Mitaru was grateful to be given this mission.

He'd been feeling displaced and adrift, with no goals tethering him to the world around him, ever since his unit had failed in their one sacred duty as Guardians of the Veil.

Even worse, he was worried about Luna and Zara.

He'd come to realize how selfish he'd been, to become a Guardian at all.

He'd comforted himself with the knowledge that his sisters would be cherished by the Fae, for their sacrifice and for his.

He hadn't given a single thought to what it would be like for them, emotionally, when he was gone.

Or if he had, he'd brushed it aside, not to be truly faced until it was entirely too late.

In fact, if all had gone as planned, he'd never have had to face it at all, for he'd have been gone and any suffering his sisters endured would have been beyond his understanding.

Yet, here he was.

On the mortal side of the Veils.

Separated from his sisters as expected, but still part of this world.

Unable to stop thinking about them, worrying about them.

All of it made infinitely worse for having lost his direction.

A Guardian still, yet without a purpose.

Untethered.

Far from home.

A failure, with nothing to do but worry about his sisters' fate.

Then came this mission, given to them by Princess Astra herself, assigning him a purpose once more.

Find Princess Glory.

Protect her with his life.

This was one mission he was determined not to fail at, though the length of time it was taking to simply reach the last known location of Princess Glory was not a good sign.

None of the Fae wished to avail themselves of mortal transport and so, they were traveling on mortal steeds, who, though worthy and valiant, were not of Faerie and thus, required greater care.

Even with a bit of Fae magic for stamina and heal-ing, they were still only managing to travel sixty to seventy miles a day. To make matters worse, they had to pause every fifth or sixth day to allow the horses time to rest and recover.

Mitaru was impatient to reach their destination, to begin searching for Princess Glory and to ensure her safety.

The more time that passed, the more anxious he became, worried about what might have befallen the princess in the intervening weeks.

Princess Astra should not have waited so long. They should have left for the northeast immediately after the Veils fell.

There was no going back though; they could only move forward and hope for the best.

The closer they got to the shield, the more Fae they encountered and the more stories they heard of Fae trying to cross the barrier to reach the Eastern Veil and failing.

They spoke of waiting for Princess Glory to come out and guide them in, but then, when she never emerged, of turning their hopes West.

They were on their way toward Princess Astra's territories when they met up with Mitaru and the rest of his unit.

They did all they could for those Fae, sharing stories of what awaited them in Kansas and providing guidance on where to stop and rest as they journeyed west.

These stops to converse with other Fae also delayed their travels and so, Mitaru and his unit were well into their fourth week of travel by the time they arrived at the shield.

It was an amazing sight.

There were encampments all along the banks of a river for as far as the eye could see, and just beyond them, rising from the waters, was a barrier Mitaru instantly recognized as a construct of Faerie. It fairly glowed with Fae magic and seemed to stretch into eternity.

"Is that the Potomac?" Kalina's mate, Thorne, asked.

"Must be," Kalina said. "I didn't expect the shield to be so grand. It's huge compared to the one in Lawrence. Strange, don't you think?"

"Very," Thorne answered.

"How are we going to get inside?" Mitaru asked impatiently. He didn't care about the barrier's size. He simply wanted to reach the princess as soon as possible.

"I'll be honest," Thorne said. "I doubt it can be done."

Mitaru refused to believe that. "If that were true, why did we bother traveling here at all?"

"The Princess commands. We comply," Kalina said. "It's as simple as that. Unfortunately, Thorne is right. I cannot imagine that we will be able to accomplish what so many Fae we've encountered along the journey have not."

"None of the Fae we met were Guardians of the Veil."

"He has a point," Thorne said.

"Yes, but the Veil isn't letting any of us cross back into Faerie. Why would this barrier be any different?"

"Well, we're not going to accomplish anything by just talking about it," Jeniah spoke up.

Mitaru nodded. "Yes, we need to at least try."

"Let's go then." Kalina led the way down the slight incline toward the Fae encampment.

It took them almost the entire afternoon to make it through the encampment to the bank of the river itself.

"Supposedly there's a bridge over there somewhere." One of the Fae gestured vaguely in the distance. "Problem is no one can see it. I guess all the bridges are behind the barrier."

"Well, that's not exactly helpful." Mitaru nudged his mount forward and with a bit of Fae magic, encouraged the horse to enter the waters of the Potomac.

Despite his efforts, though, the horse didn't exactly plunge forward. Instead, he moved with slow, plodding steps before coming to a halt a few feet in and refusing to budge.

Mitaru sighed.

"Are you serious right now?" Kalina exclaimed from behind him.

Mitaru glanced back and shook his head at the sight of her mount backing away from the murky waters.

"The river's disgusting," Kalina called to him. "I can't believe you convinced the horse to enter it."

"We're Fae, for fate's sake!" Mitaru exclaimed. "Use your magic. Convince the horse."

"That's not exactly kind to the horse," Thorne pointed out. "In fact, it might be considered a bit cruel."

Mitaru groaned. "Come on, guys. Princess Glory is counting on us."

"For all we know, she's fine," Kalina said.

"For all we know, she's dead," Thorne muttered.

For some reason, those words enraged Mitaru, to the point he barely yanked back his magic in time.

From the look on Thorne's face, the other Guardian had a pretty good idea how close he'd come to being knocked clean off his horse.

"You know, the humans claim the river's the cleanest it's been in decades," a Fae from the encampment said.

Mitaru grimaced. How was that even possible? "Look, you guys can try to find the bridge if you want, but this is the fastest route and I'm taking it."

"How do you know it's the fastest?" Kalina demanded.

"I just do." Mitaru leaned over his horse, stroked a hand down his neck and sent a soothing wave of magic through him. He nodded in satisfaction when the horse began moving forward again, making his way deeper into the water.

Behind him, Kalina groaned in exasperation and Mitaru grinned. She might order the rest of the Guardians to stay behind, but he knew Kalina would never allow her best friend to step into an unknown situation alone.

Which meant he'd have at least two Fae at his back, for Thorne Evaria would never leave his mate behind.

Mitaru glanced back in time to see a wave of magic that began at the bank of the river ripple through the waters, sweeping sludge and pollution away from where Kalina and the other Guardians stood, forging a path toward Mitaru.

"Zerika, you're the best!" Kalina exclaimed, grinning at their fellow Guardian who had the ability to heal.

Mitaru would have never expected that ability to transfer to a river, but it made sense. The river, like all parts of the natural world, was a living entity that could be both harmed and healed.

Kalina urged her horse into the Potomac and the rest of the Guardians followed.

As they neared where Mitaru was waiting, Kalina waved Zerika forward.

Zerika sent a ripple of her magic through the

waters, clearing another path, this time headed straight for the barrier.

The horses seemed invigorated by the now-clean waters and surged forward, swimming toward the barrier with a renewed sense of energy and purpose.

Mitaru reached the barrier first and without pause plunged straight through it.

It was the strangest barrier of Faerie he'd ever crossed.

Every other passage was simply like stepping through a doorway, one moment in Faerie, the next in the mortal realm.

This barrier though did not divide Faerie from the mortal world, but rather the mortal world from itself.

And yet, it felt like Mitaru had entered Faerie.

A strange and foreign Faerie.

The horse he rode let out a whinny of distress and Mitaru crooned to him softly, sending another ripple of soothing magic through him.

Mitaru glanced back, but couldn't see Kalina, Thorne or any of the other Guardians. He also couldn't see the waters he could feel against his legs as the horse powered through them.

Everything around them had been erased by a strange fog that felt dense with the magic of Faerie.

Mitaru faced forward again.

He could only hope that somewhere in the fog the other Guardians followed.

One moment, they were still in the water, the next they were climbing onto the bank on the other side of the river.

The horse stumbled and went down.

Mitaru leapt free of the horse and fell to his knees beside him.

The horse was still breathing and didn't seem to have any injuries.

Yet his eyes were closed and he wasn't moving.

At that moment, two other horses arrived on the bank, appearing from the fog as if by magic.

Two steps onto land and both horses toppled to the side.

From Mitaru's perspective, it was as if an invisible hand reached out and slowly lowered them to the ground, for neither horse fell at a speed consistent with gravity.

Instead they fell as if in slow motion, settling on the ground silently.

Both Thorne and Kalina leapt free of their mounts, then did as Mitaru had. They verified the horses were still breathing, then glanced at Mitaru in confusion.

He shrugged. "I don't know. They appear to be sleeping. Where are the others?"

Kalina faced the river. "They were right behind us."

Mitaru stood and for the first time took a look around.

They stood on the grassy bank of the river and not too far from where they stood— "Found the bridge."

Kalina followed his gaze and scowled. "Figures."

Only part of the bridge could be seen, rising from the water, the majority of it disappearing into the foggy mist as if it weren't truly there.

"I'm not sure they're coming," Thorne interrupted, eyes focused on where he and Kalina had emerged from the mist. "I can't see a thing."

"It's been too long," Mitaru said.

"You two wait here." Kalina started for the river.

"I'll go with you," Thorne said.

"We'll all go," Mitaru said. "It doesn't make sense to separate at this point."

"I just need to make sure they're okay."

"They probably never made it past the barrier," Thorne said.

"If that's the case, then maybe we shouldn't go back," Mitaru said, worried they wouldn't be able to make the crossing again.

"Just wait here," Kalina repeated, then plunged forward and disappeared into the mist.

Thorne let out a growl of anger. "I can't believe she just went without us."

"That's Kalina for you," Mitaru said. "She's not going to let anyone take a risk she won't take first."

"She still should have waited for us, taken us with her." Thorne paced back and forth. "If she's not back in another minute, I'm—" He broke off in surprise when Kalina reappeared.

She strode toward them, shoving back her wet hair. "They're all on the other side of the barrier. I told them to head back to Lawrence, that there was no point in them just hanging out at the barrier since it wouldn't let them through."

"Wait. You already spoke with them?" Thorne demanded.

Kalina nodded. "It took me a lot longer this time to get through the fog to the barrier and for a moment, I thought it wasn't going to let me through again, but it did, though the magic felt heavier this time around."

"You made it all the way to the barrier, spoke with the other Guardians and swam back here?" Thorne repeated.

Kalina nodded. "I knew it was taking longer than before, but I had no idea how long until the other Guardians told me they'd been watching the barrier all day, waiting for us to reappear."

"All day?" Thorne and Mitaru exclaimed together.

"I know. Crazy, right? It felt like maybe an hour or two from my perspective."

"You weren't even gone that long," Thorne protested.

"You'd barely left when you reappeared," MItaru agreed. "It couldn't have taken more than a minute or two."

"That does not bode well for this journey," Kalina said.

"Not if time is moving differently this side of the barrier," Thorne said.

"All right, let's get moving," Mitaru interrupted. He was getting anxious, filled with a rising sense of urgency to find Princess Glory.

"I guess we're on foot," Kalina said.

CHAPTER 3

INSIDE THE NORTHEASTERN SHIELD

*M*itaru wasn't surprised to discover a set of concrete steps and a road not far from the bank of the river.

He was getting used to the cities of the mortals, where they tended to cover the natural with ugly constructions that were mortal-made. Used to them, though, didn't mean he liked them.

In fact, the entire trip from Lawrence, Kansas, to Washington, D.C. had been frustrating as the Fae attempted to find routes that allowed them to walk across the natural earth, but instead, more often than not, found themselves walking along unnatural, mortal-made roads.

As a result, Mitaru wasn't at all surprised to discover Washington, D.C. had as much concrete as any other city they'd passed through. Despite the familiarity, though, the city felt strange.

There was a quiet in the air that felt unnatural.

"There's no wind," Kalina remarked as they climbed the concrete steps and started across the first road.

She was right. It wasn't the only indication that something wasn't right, though.

"No birds in the sky," Thorne said.

Mitaru looked up. He hadn't really noticed, but now that Thorne had pointed it out, the lack of birds was as eerie as the silence.

Then they came across the first vehicle.

The vehicle itself was nothing new.

They had encountered many cars and trucks along the roads they'd traveled, but these particular vehicles were different.

They might be on the roads, but they weren't moving.

They weren't stopped at lights or stop signs either.

Nor were they parked along the sides of the road.

Instead, they simply sat in the middle of it, abandoned.

As Mitaru got closer to the first one, he realized a mortal was still seated inside.

So not abandoned after all.

"What's going on?" Kalina asked in a hushed voice at his side.

Mitaru shook his head, walked up to the driver's side of the car and knocked on the window.

The woman inside didn't move.

"Has she passed into eternity?" Thorne asked.

"I can't tell." Mitaru opened the car door and leaned in. "I think she's asleep, like the horses." He waved a hand in front of her face, but she didn't flinch.

"Her eyes are open," Kalina observed from where she stood at the front of the car.

"Maybe she's just frozen," Thorne said.

"With time slowed inside the shield, that would make perfect sense," Mitaru said, closing the car door and glancing around, taking note of the other cars with mortals inside them.

"Then why aren't we frozen?" Kalina demanded.

It was a good question, but not one Mitaru knew how to answer. "We should keep moving."

He strode around the car and ignoring the cars in the next lane, hurried to the base of another set of concrete stairs, these much wider and taller, and began to climb.

"That's disturbing," Kalina muttered as they passed a mortal, frozen mid-step, heading down the stairs, and another at the top of the stairs, in the middle of a turn, as if he was about to run back down the stairs he'd just climbed.

"Bizarre," Thorne agreed.

Feeling an increasing sense of urgency, Mitaru picked up the pace, hurrying across two additional roads, weaving in and out of the cars there, until he reached another grassy area and broke into a run.

Somewhere beyond this grassy area, beyond the building with towering pillars to their left, they would find Princess Glory. He just knew it.

It didn't take long, with the pace Mitaru set for them to reach the area the mortals called the National Mall.

Mitaru had learned that the mortals referred to inside shopping areas as malls, but that in this case, in the capitol city of Washington, D.C., the mall referred to something else.

This particular mall featured museums and monuments, fountains and a mortal-made pool among other things.

It was at this pool where the Eastern Veil was located and where Princess Glory, along with all the other Fae accompanying her, had last been seen.

Mitaru knew they were in the right place when they came upon the guardian force of the mortals.

Soldiers and police, they called them.

"They still have their weapons," Thorne warned as they slipped through the frozen mortals.

"We should disarm them," Kalina said. "They cannot be trusted."

Despite Mitaru's desperation to find Glory, he absolutely agreed as he had no desire to be shot again.

"We should try to use the magic of Faerie," Thorne said. "It worked for Astra."

"Yes, but she's a princess, tied to the magic of Faerie in a way that we are not," Mitaru protested. "I'm not sure—"

"We should at least try," Kalina said, "as I have no desire to watch you fall again, Mitaru."

The look on her face told Mitaru how much the events in Lawrence had impacted her.

He didn't remember much about what had happened, just of being hit by something so forceful, it seemed a thousand Sorenalaya—those Fae who had faded so far from the world of the living that they'd become nothing more than beasts—were burrowing deep, devouring his flesh and soul from the inside out.

He'd felt his life force fading, heard Kalina shouting as if from a distance and then he'd been filled with so much magic, it had felt as if his form was being burned from the inside out.

When he'd come back to the world, he'd found everything changed.

Now they all had to live with the repercussions of those changes.

"You know, standing here, from the outside looking

in," Thorne said, "I'm beginning to understand why we were met with such force back in Lawrence."

"What are you talking about?" Kalina whirled on him. "The mortals were out of control. Guardians were falling everywhere and if it weren't for Princess Astra, we'd have all entered eternity right then!"

"I understand that, Kalina, but look." Thorne nodded toward something over her shoulder.

Mitaru and Kalina turned to look and Mitaru's breath caught in his throat.

There were the Fae Guardians of the Eastern Veil, so many of them, standing in lines, facing the mortals.

Some were falling backward, others were falling to their knees while still others were already on the ground.

Many, many more, though, were standing strong, lunging forward, seconds from engaging the mortals.

Whether falling or standing or leaping forward, though, all of the Guardians—every single one—had their swords drawn.

It was a frozen battlefield, upon which the mortals were clearly outnumbered.

"There must be a hundred Guardians at least," Kalina muttered. "No wonder the mortals attacked. They probably thought they were being invaded."

"It looks like my entire generation crossed," Thorne said, staring around at the Guardians he had served with for the majority of his service to Faerie. "I recognize Guardians from every unit, but none from my brother's generation."

"Are you sure?" Mitaru asked. "Once we find Glory, we can look for Tarek as well if you'd like."

"No need. He was granted leave to be at the Western Veil when we crossed over."

"He was in our Honor Guard," Kalina said.

Mitaru didn't know whether that was a blessing or salt in the wound.

"Nako should be here though," Kalina said, referring to Thorne's best friend.

"He should," Mitaru agreed. "I'll look for him after we find the Princess. It's interesting so many of the Guardians made it through the Eastern Veil when so few did so in Lawrence.".

"Yes, but the Sorenalaya attacked at the Western Veil," Kalina said.

Mitaru winced. He couldn't believe she'd brought that up when they'd just been speaking of Tarek.

Most of the Guardians in the West had stayed behind to protect the mortal realm from the Sorenalaya. Tarek would have been no different, leaping into battle to defend the innocent, even though he was technically a Guardian of the East.

Poor Thorne didn't need any reminders of the dangers his brother had faced back home.

Then again, if Tarek had managed to survive that confrontation, at least he was also safe in Faerie right now, rather than living in exile with his brother, or worse, frozen here on this battlefield.

A battlefield that was hiding a princess.

"So, where is this infamous pool?" Mitaru asked, moving past another cluster of combatants, trying to find the area where Princess Glory had last been seen.

She'd been standing in the waters of what the mortals called the Lincoln Memorial Reflecting Pool, but everywhere Mitaru looked were black-clad Guardians of Faerie and weapon-heavy soldiers and police officers of Earth.

It took them a while to weave their way through line after line of Guardians, but they finally arrived at the Reflecting Pool.

Guardians had surrounded this end of it and from what Mitaru could see, the pool extended far beyond the section they protected.

At the center of that section, the Eastern Veil towered above the waters, providing a glimpse into Faerie.

Surrounding the Veil, a secondary cluster of Guardians faced outward, standing as Faerie's last line of defense.

Mitaru knew at the center of that cluster, not far from the Veil, would be the princess herself. He stepped into the waters and strode through them toward the Veil.

Kalina and Thorne followed.

When they reached the cluster, it became clear a hole had been punched through the Fae defenses surrounding the Veil.

It was a small hole, created by three Guardians who had fallen at the edges of the pool and another Guardian who had fallen to her knees in the water, but it was enough.

Just beyond the Guardian on her knees was the Princess.

She was half submerged in the water, not resting at the bottom of the pool, but not floating on its surface either.

She had clearly been falling and had just hit the top of the water when everything stopped.

Water had geysered up all around her.

Droplets hung in mid-air, tiny jewels that captured the light and sparked rainbows across the water.

Mitaru's heart almost stopped when he first saw her.

He had never seen anything more beautiful in all his days.

For a split second, he was frozen, unable to move at the sight of her, but then that sense of urgency came rushing back.

He slid past the Guardian on her knees and entered the protective circle that should have kept the princess safe. He splashed to her side, then knelt and slid his arms beneath her form.

Cradling her against his chest, he stood, then turned and carried her back the way he'd come, Kalina and Thorne flanking him on either side.

When they reached the edge of the pool, Kalina and Thorne exited first, then turned to help stabilize his own climb out of the waters.

Once they were on solid ground, Mitaru paused, uncertain what to do with the precious burden in his arms.

"What now?" Kalina asked.

Glory's eyes were closed as if she were unconscious or sleeping, but Mitaru could feel the magic that was actively working to hold the entire place in a form of stasis.

She was the reason everything had stopped.

"We should try to wake her, don't you think?" Thorne asked.

"If we do that, it's possible everyone else will waken," Mitaru said as he strode through the groupings of frozen Fae and mortals. He needed to get her away from where all those weapons were pointing.

"Wait. Are you saying it's *Glory's* magic that's caused

all this?" Kalina demanded as Mitaru reached a grassy area far from where the confrontation was happening.

He lowered himself to his knees, then gently lay the Princess on the ground.

He brushed aside a lock of hair that had fallen across her cheek, tucking it tenderly behind one ear.

Kalina and Thorne settled on the other side of Glory and stared at him, perplexed looks on their faces.

"I can feel her magic," Mitaru said. "It's all wrapped up and twined together with the magic of Faerie."

"Like Astra's magic," Kalina said.

Mitaru nodded.

"I don't know why I'm surprised," Thorne said. "She *is* a Fae Royal just like her sister."

"Well, before we wake her, we need to secure the area," Mitaru said. "Once the magic has disbanded, that battle—" He gestured toward where the Fae and mortals faced off. "—could begin anew."

"Right. Weapons first," Thorne declared.

"Weapons first," Kalina agreed.

Mitaru didn't want to leave the princess, but part of protecting her was ensuring that none of the mortals in her vicinity were armed.

He climbed to his feet and followed Kalina and Thorne back onto the battlefield.

CHAPTER 4

They started with the mortals.

Or at least they tried to.

It didn't take long for them to discover that none of them had the ability to disarm the mortals *or* the Fae.

"Maybe it's because they're frozen?" Kalina suggested.

"The magic *does* seem to be making this more diffi-cult," Thorne said. "It's like it's working against us."

"I still say we should—" Mitaru caught his breath. Had she just—

He bolted through a cluster of Guardians, slid around another line of them and raced toward the grassy knoll where they'd left Glory's body.

He fell to his knees at her side. Fear and hope

warring in his heart, he attempted to open a pathway. *Glory?*

No response.

Kalina and Thorne arrived an instant later.

"What is it?" Kalina asked sharply.

"I'm not sure. Her heart skipped a beat." *Glory, wake up!*

"You heard it?" Thorne asked.

Mitaru shook his head. "I felt it." *Come on, Glory. I know you're in there.*

"That's not good," Kalina said.

"Well, this is strange."

The three of them looked up at the new voice.

For a split second, Mitaru's heart stopped, thinking the princess—his mate?—had turned into one of the Sorenalaya.

But no.

Although she was transparent like one of the Fae who had faded from the world, she was still as beautiful as ever. She was not rail thin nor did she have the claws and fangs of the lost.

"What—what do you think you're doing?" Mitaru exclaimed as he surged to his feet.

He glared at Glory who stood across from him, hands on hips, staring down at herself. "Get back in your body right now!"

"Well, it's not like I did it on purpose, now is it?"

Glory snapped. "I'm not sure how I got out of my body, let alone how to get back in it."

Mitaru was speechless. Glancing at Kalina and Thorne, he saw they were the same.

"We've not met," Glory said to Mitaru. Without waiting for a reply, she continued, "But I do know you two. Kalina Wyendeh and Thorne Evaria, our Guardian mates. You were quite the unexpected surprise."

"Princess Glory, it is nice to see you again," Kalina said.

Throne murmured an agreement, a worried look on his face.

Mitaru knew exactly how he felt. "Would you at least *attempt* to get back in your body now?"

Glory just looked at him.

"*Please.*" He was feeling a little desperate, though he wasn't sure why. He just didn't like that she stood there in front of them, insubstantial as one of the Faded, her body at their feet filling him with dread.

"I will if you will tell me your name."

"Mitaru Verushi at your service." He swept an arm toward her body. "If you would, my Princess."

Glory stepped over to her body, though it would perhaps be more accurate to say she glided toward it, then carefully lowered herself so that she settled inside her body, each part of her insubstantial form disappearing into the corresponding physical one.

Mitaru waited impatiently for her to open her eyes.

Nothing happened.

"Why isn't she waking up?" Kalina sounded as worried as Mitaru felt.

"Because it's not working." Glory climbed back out of her body. "I'm not sure why I can't seem to stick to my flesh and bones, but I can't. Is my body still breathing?"

Mitaru leaned over and set his fingers against the pulse in Glory's neck. "You're still alive. You just seem to be unconscious or sleeping."

"I am *not* sleeping. If I were asleep, I'm sure the three of you towering over me would have awakened me by now." She glanced around, seeming to just then realize her body wasn't where she'd last left it. "Where are we anyway?" She turned in a circle and took in the sight of the humans and Guardians standing frozen around them. "And why are you three the only ones moving around here?"

"We were hoping you could tell us that," Mitaru said.

"Me?"

"Do you not feel the magic in the air?" Kalina asked. "It's Faerie magic, wild and completely unleashed in this space."

Glory looked stricken. "That's not possible. I keep that magic locked down tight *always*."

"I'm thinking you didn't have a choice," Mitaru

said. He'd just noticed something he recognized, something that filled him with a rage so vast he was afraid for a split second that he was about to turn feral.

He clamped down on the raging beast inside him and sank to his knees beside the Princess' body.

"What is it, Mitaru?" Kalina asked.

"I think she's been shot." He reached out with a trembling hand and smoothed the tunic Glory was wearing to the side, revealing the rest of the jagged starburst he hadn't noticed until now.

It was high on her chest, above where the tunic would have rested.

He had similar starbursts on his left shoulder, front and back, as well as a third one in the middle of his torso.

The bullets had torn through his body with a force he'd never experienced and the pain had been indescribable.

The day he'd been shot, death was already on the agenda, but it was supposed to be in sacrifice to rebuild the Veils of Faerie.

He had not expected to die at the hands of the mortals.

Yet, it had almost happened.

It was only because of Princess Astra that he still lived. She had healed everyone on that battlefield, filling them with her healing magic and he had considered it to be a miracle.

Now looking at the starburst scar on Princess Glory's chest that matched his own scars, remnants of Princess Astra's magic pouring through his body, he wondered for a split second whether her magic had managed to heal her sister a thousand miles away too.

Then he realized.

Princess Glory had healed *herself*, a feat absolutely unheard of in the entirety of Fae history.

"Why are you looking at me like that?" Glory demanded.

Mitaru looked up at her, disoriented.

He hadn't been looking at *her,* at least not the one speaking to him, but rather at her body. Still, he supposed they were both her.

Confusing.

"You healed yourself." He could see the awe that echoed in his voice on Kalina and Thorne's faces.

"What are you talking about? No one can heal themselves."

"You have a scar, the same scar I have from a bullet wound being healed by magic and not just any magic—fierce, wild magic."

"The magic of Faerie," Thorne said.

"Yes, but that doesn't mean I healed myself."

"You were the only Royal here, Princess Glory."

Kalina said. "Besides, everyone else was frozen alongside you. Not a single Fae could have helped you once you were shot, not if they were frozen when you were."

"You truly don't remember what happened?" Mitaru asked.

Glory shivered at the sight of the starburst.

She *did* remember what happened. She just didn't want to talk about it.

Or think about it.

The way that Raiyana had fallen to her knees, the pain, the loss of control.

No way to avoid it.

"Where did you find me?"

"In the Reflecting Pool," Kalina said.

"Lead me back there."

"What about your body?" Mitaru demanded. "I don't want to leave it unprotected."

"It's not like there's anyone here capable of hurting me at the moment, other than you three." Glory waved a hand. "I should be fine. Now, let's go."

"All right then." Kalina started off and Glory followed, ignoring the sound of Mitaru muttering behind them.

There was something about that Fae that made her skin itch, except she had no skin in this form, so maybe he just made her soul itch, which when she thought about it, was infinitely worse.

She wanted to wrap herself around him and get as far away from him as possible, all at the same time.

It made no sense.

Just as this frozen tableau made no sense.

Humans with weapons everywhere pointed at Fae Guardians with swords drawn.

There were even bullets mid-air that she could see would have hit the Fae in seconds had everything not just stopped.

As they walked through the frozen battlefield, she pinched tiny pockets of magic all around her and flicked it at the combatants, destroying the weapons the humans held, disintegrating bullets everywhere and sheathing the swords of the Fae.

From where it started, the magic continued its sweep, winding its way through the frozen scene, spreading ever outward, destroying and sheathing weapons in its wake.

This was good.

Glory had no idea if she would be able to reign back the wild magic she had apparently unleashed while unconscious—that feral magic that had frozen everyone in its vicinity—but at least now, if she did manage the impossible, the battle that had started everything would have ended while the world was sleeping.

"We found you over there, just inside the circle of your Royal Guard, by the Veil." Kalina pointed toward the center of the Reflecting Pool.

"We should collect any bullets that fell in the pool and purge it of magical blood." Mitaru pushed his way past the two of them and stepped into the waters. "We cannot allow the mortals even one drop of the blood of the Fae."

"Agreed," Thorne said. "This pool is huge though and who knows how far the blood may have traveled. We'll need to start at the far end and work our way back this way."

As the two males headed off on their self-appointed task, Glory climbed into the pool and made her way toward where Raiyana had fallen.

The Fae Guardian was on her knees still.

No.

As Glory came closer, she saw that Raiyana had not quite made it all the way down to her knees. Most of the way down, yes, but still perhaps an inch from the bottom of the pool.

There was a giant hole in the front of Raiyana's tunic and a slightly smaller one in the back. Where the wounds should be, there were two starburst scars instead.

"They're larger than mine."

"Different weapons perhaps," Kalina said. "They appear to be healed though, like yours."

The relief Glory felt was indescribable.

She quickly walked in a circle, taking in the status of the rest of her Guard.

They had all surrounded her in the pool, she remembered now, blocking her view of what had been happening.

"The mortals attacked and we started to fall." She glared around. Several of her Guard had fallen and beyond them, many more Guardians were in the process of falling as well. "Why did we fall so quickly?"

"The mortal weapons allow them to attack at a distance and they can fire many bullets all at once. They would have been able to take down many in a heartbeat."

Glory closed her eyes and sent her consciousness outward, checking on the many Fae she felt responsible for.

"What are you doing?" Kalina exclaimed, her voice coming as if from a great distance. "You're fading! Stop that!"

Glory's eyes snapped open. "I was just reaching out

to see if any of the Fae are still injured. I think they have all been healed."

"Well, don't do that again. You looked like you might disappear at any moment."

"Fine." Glory sighed. "Apparently the magic decided to heal the humans as well, even though they are not worthy of Fae magic."

"We far outnumbered the humans here, Princess Glory," Kalina said. "They probably thought we were invading."

"Yes, well, the Fae would never have drawn swords on mortals had they not been attacked, maybe not even then if it weren't for their need to protect the entrance to Faerie. So, say what you will, Kalina, this entire situation is the humans' fault."

"Yes, the humans. The ones who were clearly outnumbered and undoubtedly terrified."

Glory scowled. She didn't want to hear the humans' excuses and certainly not from a Fae.

The problem was that Kalina was right, though Glory hated to admit it.

The truth was this was entirely the Fae's fault.

Though Glory understood why the Guardians of the Eastern Veil had crossed into mortal lands—when the Veil had fallen, their one and only duty was to guard the entrance of Faerie—but their actions had no doubt been seen as an act of war by the mortals and thus, were the true catalyst for everything that had happened since.

In hindsight, there were probably better ways for the Fae to have responded to the fall of the Veil.

The problem was they simply weren't prepared. No one had expected the Veil to fall or for the Fae themselves to be Unveiled to the humans.

The result was this chaos and Glory had no idea how to fix it.

At that moment, Thorne and Mitaru returned.

Glory had been aware of their magic rippling through the waters around them, not just cleansing them of Fae blood—there had been no bullets for their magic to find, of course—but also of all manner of chemicals and unnatural substances.

When the magic had reached the waters around the Veil, though, it had only found blood. No chemicals or pollution to mar the purity of the water.

It wasn't surprising really.

The lands directly around the Veils were always cleaner and healthier than those further out. It was almost as if a bit of Faerie magic trickled over onto the earth side to heal the area closest to Faerie.

This was always a bit disturbing to Glory as it made her concerned the reverse could also be true: that the mortal world, with its unnatural chemicals, concrete cities and dying wildlife could somehow cross into Faerie and then their lands would be dying too.

"The waters have been cleansed for the most part," Thorne reported.

"We just need to get everyone out of the pool so that we can do one last sweep," Mitaru said, "just to ensure we leave nothing of Faerie behind."

"Well, that's going to be an impossible task," Glory said, "considering we can't exactly relocate the Veil."

"We can try to hide it though, right?" Thorne asked.

"It won't do any good," Glory said. "Once mortal eyes have seen the truth, it is almost impossible to keep them from seeing it again, especially if they have accepted as truth what their eyes have seen."

"So there's nothing to be done?" Kalina asked.

"The best I can do is create a shield around the Veil, basically barring mortals from crossing it."

"Like what Astra did in Lawrence," Mitaru said.

"Astra?" Glory whirled on Mitaru. "You've seen my sister?"

CHAPTER 5

It took hours for them to relocate Princess Glory's Royal Guard from inside the Reflecting Pool to outside it and then to cleanse the pool. While they worked, Mitaru, Kalina and Thorne updated Princess Glory on the happenings in Lawrence, Kansas, where the Western Veil had fallen and where Princess Astra had established a tiny bit of Faerie to serve as home for the many displaced Fae.

"We should go there," Princess Glory decided.

"Go where?" Kalina asked.

"West, to this Lawrence, Kansas, where my sister and all the Fae are gathering."

"You don't wish to claim these lands the way that Astra is claiming the lands of Kansas?" Thorne asked.

"There is no way the mortals would see that as

anything less than an act of war. This is their capitol city in this part of the world." She waved an arm around them. "We are surrounded by memorials to their mortal Guardians who fought to defend them and died in wars long past. We cannot take this space from the mortals."

"How do you know all this?" Mitaru asked.

"I traveled here with my Royal Guard a couple weeks ago. We walked the space to ensure we knew exactly where we would arrive and what we would be facing. This location is much changed from five hundred years ago when the last Ceremony of the Veils occurred. I was intrigued at the changes and so we spent the day exploring what the mortals call their National Mall."

"Isn't a mall a shopping center?" Thorne asked.

"I thought the same thing," Glory said. "But apparently not in Washington, D.C. Here, a mall is not for shopping, but for museums and monuments and fountains and memorials. They may not be made of nature, but they were certainly made from the heart and so we will not take these places from the mortals."

"So what's the plan then?" Mitaru demanded. "Your body is still lying over there, vulnerable and without your essence inside it. We cannot leave this location for the mortals until you reintegrate."

"And our people wake up," Kalina agreed.

"So let's start there," Glory said. "Time to wake our people."

"You know how?" Thorne asked.

Glory stopped before a Guardian of the Eastern Veil. His arms were held out, loose fists at the ready, telling Glory that he had been holding both of his swords at the time everything froze.

Now he was unarmed, both swords sheathed by the magic once more.

It couldn't be too hard, she didn't think, to find the magic that held him to sleep and nudge it toward wakefulness.

She closed her eyes and reached out with her magic.

"You're doing that thing again!" Kalina exclaimed.

"What thing?" Mitaru's voice came as if from a distance. "Hey! Glory, stop that. Snap out of it."

Glory's consciousness had traveled far, but the feel of Mitaru's hand snapping round her wrist, which shouldn't be possible—her body and spirit were not connected at the moment—yanked her back.

Her eyes flew open. "The magic that's holding them all asleep is interconnected. If I wake one of the Guardians, I will wake them all."

"Will it wake the humans?" Kalina asked, a practical question Glory appreciated.

"I'm not sure." Glory turned away from the

Guardian and walked up to the mortal he was mere feet from engaging.

She sent her consciousness edging out again, but didn't get very far before Mitaru snatched her back with a quick squeeze of her neck.

"How are you doing that?" She whirled on him.

"Doing what?"

"Touching my body when it's over there and you're over here."

"You touched the Princess?" Thorne sounded shocked.

"Not like that!" Mitaru protested. "She was traveling too far from us so I grabbed her wrist."

"And my neck."

"But she isn't in her body at the moment," Kalina said. "She shouldn't have felt anything."

"And yet, I did." Glory glared at Mitaru, who sketched a quick bow.

"My apologies, Princess." The tone of his voice wasn't very apologetic, nor was his bow very respectful. So quick and shallow as to almost be pointless.

Glory narrowed her eyes at him. Why did this Guardian annoy her so? Her skin prickled where he'd touched it. She rubbed her wrist, then reached up toward her neck, but when she saw he was watching, quickly dropped her hand.

She turned from him and said to Kalina, "The magic

holding the Guardians asleep is not connected to the mortals. I can wake the Fae without disturbing the humans."

"Fantastic. So let's do it," Thorne said impatiently. "I want to find Nako."

"First, the Veil, then our people, then we retreat from these lands," Glory said. "Once most of our people are outside the shield, on their way to my sister, I will release the magic holding the humans asleep."

"No," Mitaru said. "First, you must reintegrate with your body."

"I told you—I don't know how!"

"You're rubbing your wrist," Kalina said.

"What?"

"Your wrist. You're rubbing it."

Glory glanced down at her hands and realized Kalina was right. She was rubbing her wrist again. And now that she was paying attention, she realized she could actually feel both hands.

She closed her eyes and tried to tune into her body, but no, the rest of it was still numb.

Except for the two spots on her neck where Mitaru had placed his fingers and squeezed.

Those spots tingled.

"I have feeling in my hands again," Glory said, "but the rest of me is still numb."

"May I?" Kalina reached out a hand toward Glory's shoulder.

Glory nodded.

Kalina touched Glory's shoulder, but Glory felt nothing.

"You're not really there," Kalina said. "My hand passes right through your shoulder. How did you grab her wrist when she doesn't have a physical form?"

Mitaru shrugged. "I'm not sure."

"Well, try it again," Thorne urged.

Mitaru reached for the same shoulder Kalina had attempted to touch.

His hand was warm and that warmth seeped through Glory's shoulder, making her realize how achingly cold she was.

He squeezed her shoulder and her breath caught.

What was it about this Fae, that he could somehow touch her soul and have her feel it?

"Well?" Kalina demanded.

"I'm touching her shoulder," Mitaru reported.

"And I can feel it," Glory said. "I have no idea what it means though."

Mitaru snorted.

"What?"

"You cannot possibly be that—"

"That what?"

"Oblivious."

Glory was pretty certain that *wasn't* the word he'd been about to say. "Just what are you implying?"

He grinned. "Never mind. Let's just focus on getting you reintegrated, shall we?"

"Excellent idea." Kalina had a huge grin on her face.

Glory glanced at Thorne and saw he was smiling as well. What did these three know that she didn't?

She glared at Mitaru who just held his hands up in a gesture of innocence.

"Let's go back to your body. See if we can work some magic, shall we?"

"Fine." Glory turned and stalked back through the battlefield toward the grassy area where they'd left her body.

She still lay on the ground, utterly still, no sign of waking anytime soon.

Mitaru stepped up next to Glory and they stood there, staring down at her sleeping form.

"I don't know what to do," Glory admitted. "I'm not sure how I got separated in the first place, so I really don't know how to reintegrate myself."

"Personally, I've always been a fan of mortal fairy tales," Thorne said from where he and Kalina stood on the other side of Glory's body.

"What are you talking about?" Kalina demanded.

"My mother spent many years traveling the mortal realm in her youth and she came back with a number of human fairy tales to share. One of my favorites was always Sleeping Beauty."

"I'm not familiar with it," Glory said.

"Nor am I," Kalina said.

Mitaru just shook his head.

"Basically, an evil witch casts a spell, a young princess is sent to sleep and the only way she can wake is through true love's kiss. It takes a hundred years, but eventually her true love finds her and wakes her with that kiss."

"That's ridiculous," Glory said. "How can he be her true love if she's been asleep for a hundred years? Unless they were both Fae, he's probably significantly younger than her and thus, has never even met her."

"Not the point of the story," Thorne said.

"And what about consent?" Kalina demanded.

"Exactly! The prince just kisses while she's unconscious?" Glory exclaimed. "Someone he's never met before? What kind of fairy tale is that? A Fae would be executed for daring such a thing!"

Thorne sighed. "Again. Not the point of the story. And not the point I was making."

"Then what was your point?" Kalina demanded.

"My point is that Mitaru should try kissing Glory. Maybe it will wake her."

Glory gasped and swung around to glare at Mitaru. "You're not kissing my unconscious body!"

"That won't be necessary," Thorne said. "You felt when he touched your wrist and your neck, so I imagine he'll be able to kiss you just as easily as he touched you. So, go on, try it."

"There's no way this will work." Glory scowled. "Besides, he probably doesn't even *want* to kiss me. I'm not going to force him to kiss me just so that I can maybe—"

Her words broke off as Mitaru slid an arm around her waist, yanked her close and kissed her.

She gasped and his tongue swept inside, disintegrating her every thought.

All she could feel and taste was Mitaru.

Blood rushed in her ears as she clutched his shoulders and kissed him back.

Heat raced up and down her spine.

He slid a hand up the back of her neck, to tangle his fingers in her hair.

She gasped for breath and her eyes flew open.

CHAPTER 6

One moment Mitaru was holding his mate in his arms—his *mate,* a *princess* of Faerie—and kissing the breath out of her, the next he was holding air.

He stumbled forward and caught his balance.

He glanced down at Glory and almost collapsed in relief when he saw her eyes were open and she was staring up at him.

"My princess." He knelt beside her and helped her sit up. "How are you feeling?"

"I—" She touched her lips with trembling fingers. "I don't know."

Mitaru caught her hand in his and lifted it to his lips, where he placed a kiss in the palm of her hand, then cradled it against his cheek. "I have waited an eternity to lay eyes upon you. That you were not of flesh and bone when we first met was of no consequence. I would have you at my side in whatever form you might take, sweet mate of mine."

"Mitaru," Glory whispered.

MItaru was aware that Kalina and Thorne had stepped away to give them privacy.

"I know I am not worthy of a princess of the realm, but I will spend all my days attempting to be worthy of you, my love."

"How could a Guardian of the Veil, a Fae willing to sacrifice his life for the good of Faerie and all the Fae, not be worthy of a princess of the realm? Mitaru, I am the one who is not worthy of you."

Mitaru could barely contain the joy he felt at the acceptance that shone in Glory's eyes.

"I didn't even recognize you as my mate," Glory said. "You were an itch under the skin I couldn't even feel, but I didn't understand until now. Mitaru, forgive me for not seeing you clearly."

"There is nothing to forgive, sweet Glory." To prove it, he pulled her into his arms and kissed her again.

Long moments swirled by, but then Kalina and Thorne were there, pulling them up and apart.

"And that's enough of that," Kalina said. "We need to wake the other Guardians so that we can celebrate this mating in style."

Mitaru groaned. "Thanks a lot, Kalina."

"Hey, you made sure I had a fabulous mating cere-mony. I can only do the same for you."

"I found Nako," Thorne announced. "Would you start with him, please, Glory?"

"Of course. Lead us to him."

He wasn't far from where Glory had fallen.

In fact, Glory thought she'd seen him the day the Veils fell. He'd been there at one point, asked a question maybe.

It seemed to take forever to tap into the magic now that she was skin and flesh and bone. Much longer than it had taken when she was simply mist and so much closer to the raw power that lived inside her.

Still, she found the magic and sent it a rush of energy, asking it to waken.

Guardians began to stir all over the Mall.

Confusion reigned as they tried to figure out what had happened.

Glory sent a ripple of reassurance along the bonds that connected all of the Fae and made quick, reas-suring speeches as she moved through the crowd toward where she had left her Royal Guard.

Kalina, Thorne and his best friend, Nako, followed in her wake.

Mitaru, of course, walked at her side and she took

great delight in introducing him as her mate along the away.

"Princess Glory!" Raiyana was the first to see her and the relief upon her face made Glory realize she probably should have started with her Royal Guard as they would have panicked when they realized they no longer stood inside the Reflecting Pool and that Glory was nowhere in sight.

"I'm sorry, I'm right here, I'm right here." Glory hurried toward her Guard and exchanged quick hugs with each of them.

"What is happening? Why are the mortals frozen?" Talvenia asked.

"We've all been frozen for quite some time," Glory explained. "Mitaru, Kalina and Thorne are Guardians from the Western Veil. My sister sent them to find us, for we've been hidden behind a shield since the Veils fell. They woke me first and I woke all of you."

"I had my swords out," Xilarin said, holding out his empty hands, "but now they're sheathed."

"And I was hurt. Badly," Raiyana said. "Falling. I remember falling and seeing you—Princess, you were shot!"

"Many of us were shot, Raiyana," Glory said. "When I fell, I lost control of the magic. I think it healed all of us and froze everyone around us."

"So what now?" Xilarin asked.

"Well, unfortunately, the Veils are still closed, so there is no returning to Faerie, at least not yet. Instead, we will gather our forces and retreat. We're heading west toward Lawrence, Kansas, to join my sister and the small bit of Faerie she's creating as a sanctuary for the Fae."

"But the Veil—" one of the Guardians of the Eastern Veil protested. "We're supposed to protect it. We can't just leave it."

"I'm afraid this Veil is no longer under Fae control, at least not on the mortal side of the realm. We will erect a shield to protect it and we will leave these territories for the mortals."

"What if they breach Faerie?"

"It will never happen. The magic of Faerie will keep them out. Besides, do not forget that the next two generations of Guardians serve on the Faerie side. They will continue to defend Faerie and its Veils as they have always done."

Glory used magic to project her voice through the crowds. "Guardians, prepare to migrate."

"You do not wish to have the Ceremony here before we travel?" Kalina asked.

"Ceremony?" Talvenia asked.

Glory smiled, grabbed Mitaru's hand and pulled him forward. "This is my mate, Mitaru Verushi."

The worried looks that had settled on everyone's

faces cleared as smiles broke out in response to the news.

"Congratulations, Princess Glory!" Raiyana exclaimed, her words echoed by the many Guardians around them.

"Kalina, you said there are many Fae trapped here in the mortal realm, making their way toward Lawrence, right?" Glory asked.

"Yes, we met many on our journey here."

"I'm sure those Fae and all the others trapped here in the mortal realm would appreciate the chance to attend our celebration. More, they probably need the joy and hope it would provide." Glory glanced at Mitaru, who looked pained, but nodded in agreement. He was probably just then coming to the realization of what it would mean to be the mate of a princess of the realm.

The good of the Fae would always come first.

"Therefore, our mating celebration will take place in Lawrence, so that all of the Fae might celebrate with us."

Kalina grinned. "This is going to be an epic mating celebration!"

"Right, so we need to get organized and start moving. Raiyana, please find Yerendei. He's a Guardian, but also a true artist with his magic. Have him weave us a banner worthy of the Fae.

"Kalina, I don't suppose we have any horses available?"

Kalina grinned. "As it happens, I know where three are sleeping at the moment."

"Excellent. We'll need to wake them, then I want you and Thorne to lead the procession out of the city toward our new home."

"We can't leave you," Kalina protested. "Princess Astra sent us to protect you."

"You and Thorne are the best choice for this task as you have made the journey before. Besides, I will have my Royal Guard with me. Protecting me is their duty. I will also have at my side my first protector, my mate, Mitaru."

Kalina looked stricken, which made Glory remember that Kalina had referred to Mitaru as her best friend.

"We will be the last to leave the city," Glory said gently. "It has to be that way because I am the only one who can pull the magic back, so that this city might live again."

"It's not just this city," Kalina said. "The magic has traveled north quite a distance and a bit to the southwest as well."

"And I will make sure they all waken before we leave," Glory assured her. "I promise we will make it out and we will all make it to our new home. You will see

Mitaru and me again and you will dance at our mating celebration."

Kalina sighed. "You do realize the mortals may react very badly to our appearance outside the shield."

"And that is why every Fae who walks through the shield shall take a portion of it with them—the part that provides them with a shield rather than the one that sends them to sleep."

"You can make that happen?" Mitaru asked.

"I believe so, yes."

Mitaru nodded, a thoughtful look on his face.

"Are you certain of this plan, Princess Glory?" Kalina asked. "It might not be advisable for us to split up."

"It's the best option we have," Glory said.

"Very well." Kalina stepped toward Mitaru, then hesitated.

"Go ahead." Glory nodded. She watched closely as Kalina hugged Mitaru and wished him blessings upon their journey.

They were almost like brother and sister, the way they interacted. There was no chemistry between them, yet with her mating to Mitaru not yet fulfilled, Glory did not like watching him embrace another.

Still, she held tight to her control and once their goodbyes were finished, nodded farewells to both Kalina and Thorne, whom she noted didn't look at all bothered by the shared hug. Perhaps because his mating *was* complete and he was secure in his relationship with Kalina.

Mitaru caught Glory's hand in his, threaded their fingers together and squeezed. "That was very well-done of you," he murmured. "Thank you for remembering how much we mean to each other and for allowing us to say goodbye. We all know anything could go wrong between here and Lawrence. This was important to her, to me as well."

"*You* are important to me, so I could do nothing less than give you what you need."

He lifted their hands, placed a kiss on the back of hers, then said, "What next, my princess?"

"We prepare to ride."

CHAPTER 7

NEWLY FORMED FAE TERRITORIES

Lawrence, Kansas

"Princess Astra, something's happening at the Eastern barrier!" Dyranel burst into the room where Kahji and Astra were poring over a map of the territories beyond their borders, trying to identify where next to travel to continue healing the lands and waters of the mortal earth.

The rest of Astra's Royal Guard followed him.

"Is it Glory?" A mix of terror and hope swirled inside, making Astra feel nauseous.

"We're not sure." Zanzor touched the wall across from where Astra and Kahji stood. He quickly typed the web address of a news station in the Fae browser that appeared and tapped enter. When the news station's home page loaded, he pressed the play button and everyone fell silent.

"It's been eighteen months since the Unveiling, when the world discovered there are Fae living just beyond the Veils that separate our world from theirs," the reporter on the wall announced.

"In those eighteen months, the Fae have laid claim to large portions of the earth, erecting shields around those territories. Ireland lost a small portion of land at Knock Áine and Australia lost a portion of its ocean and beaches at The Twelve Apostles in Victoria.

"However, the nation that has lost the most territory to the Fae remains the United States of America. This nation has had to learn to live without its capitol city, much of its national government, the Big Apple and the vast majority of territories in Kansas, Nebraska, Oklahoma and Missouri.

"Despite those massive land claims, travel in the midwest has been largely unaffected. As long as humans do not attempt to harm any Fae, they have been allowed to travel back and forth behind the shield without issue.

"However, here at the Eastern shield, a shield that has claimed territory from Washington, D.C. to New York City, there has been no movement from inside these territories since they were first surrounded eighteen months ago.

"We have heard tales of three Fae who journeyed here and managed somehow to enter behind the shield two months after it was erected, but we have heard no word of those Fae since. Until today, it has been assumed that these territories and everyone inside them have been lost.

"An hour ago, though, we received word that movement has been sighted just beyond the shield on Arlington Memorial Bridge. As our viewers know, the shield that encompasses Washington, D.C., erases the entirety of the bridge from view. You have to actually know that it's there to find it. We do know it's there, though, and sometimes on a sunny day, you can barely make out the outline of the bridge, if you squint and look closely."

The camera zoomed in on a space that mostly looked like mist hovering above the Potomac River, but Astra could see what the reporter was talking about.

There in the mist, figures seemed to be shifting back and forth.

"Something's happening!" The reporter said breathlessly, but the narration was unnecessary.

Everyone watching could see.

Two figures on horseback appeared, the mist peeling away as they rode forward.

At their back, there came endless lines of Fae.

They marched in units of twenty–five, in columns of five by five.

"The Guardians of the Eastern Veil," Andri whispered.

Astra blinked back tears as she stepped closer to watch.

Kahji stepped up behind her, slid an arm around her waist and pulled her close so that her back was nestled against his front. "Is that—"

She nodded. "It's Kalina and Thorne. But where is Mitaru?"

She searched the columns of Guardians as they marched forward.

A second unit of twenty-five followed the first.

Still no Mitaru.

And no Glory.

Astra couldn't even speak her name, the fear was such a huge ball of fire in the pit of her stomach.

As a third unit of Guardians emerged from the mist, the camera zoomed out so that it kept the entirety of the lines of Fae in its view.

As it did so, Kalina and Thorne came into sharp focus.

"They carry the banner of Faerie," Lumina whispered.

Kalina and Thorne rode horses, side by side, each of them holding a staff that unfurled between them the full banner of Faerie—the tree of life surrounded by the river of life, enclosed by the most sacred symbols of the ancient Fae.

It was a glorious sight, one that had a tear sliding past Astra's control.

A fourth unit marched free.

There should only be one more unit, assuming all the Guardians of this generation had crossed into D.C. before the Veils closed. Of course, if the next generation had also crossed, there could be as many as five more units to come.

"Are they safe?" Rashideh asked.

It was a good question.

Astra was surprised the mortal government hadn't shown up yet or perhaps they were already there, just not seen on the screen yet.

"If Glory's with them, they're as safe as they could ever be," Kahji said.

That, there, was the true question.

If they had Glory at their back, none would be harmed, for Glory's magic was a force unlike anything this world had ever seen, greater even than Astra's, greater even than what Glory herself had unleashed in Washington, D.C. so many months before.

Whatever Glory had done to close the rest of the world from the northeast, it was just a drop in the bucket compared to what she *could* do.

The question, then, was whether Glory had survived the magic she had already unleashed.

It seemed to Astra as if all the air had been sucked out of the room as the fifth unit marched free of the mist and everyone waited to see if anyone else would emerge.

"There!" Talveney cried out.

And there she was.

Astra chuckled as tears poured down her face. "She always did know how to make an entrance."

Glory was dressed in a gown that Astra knew she would never have worn to the Ceremony of the Veils.

Which meant she'd probably used her magic to create it for this very purpose.

This was Glory making a statement.

She looked every inch a Fae Royal—not a princess, but a queen.

She had a crown of flowers in her purple hair that she had swept up into an elaborate style with wisps falling everywhere.

The gown she wore had billowing sleeves and fell in a cascade of shimmering fabric.

She was seated upon a white horse that made the rich, purple color of her gown stand out even more. At her side was Mitaru, seated on a black horse. He was dressed entirely in black, as were her Royal Guard, who surrounded them on foot and kept pace with them as they rode slowly and regally across the Memorial Bridge.

Taken as a whole, the nine of them were a breathtaking sight as the mist retreated and Washington, D.C. was slowly Unveiled at their back.

CHAPTER 8

MORTAL TERRITORIES

It was a long journey toward their new home, made infinitely longer by the mortal government officials who kept stopping them.

They either wished to greet them joyfully and to thank them profusely for the Fae's efforts to combat the damage done to the earth or they seemed to want to arrest them.

There were even a few who pretended to want to do the first right before attempting to do the second.

They never succeeded, of course.

Glory ignored all the attempts to garner her attention and left it to her Royal Guard or the Guardians of the Veil to run interference between her and the mortals.

She was entirely too busy feeling the wounds of the earth and trying to fix as many as she could.

She'd stopped riding the horse, though she was a beautiful mount, one a Guardian of the Eastern Veil had managed to find and coax into waking from a distance.

"I just sent my magic out to find a steed worthy of a princess," the Guardian had said to Glory upon delivering the horse, who had indeed been a worthy mount.

Once they'd been traveling a few days though, Glory had realized she needed a better connection with the earth if she was going to be able to heal its pain, so she had found a mortal to return the horse to its rightful owner.

His payment?

A favor from the Fae.

It wasn't something she gave away lightly, but to ensure the horse made her way safely home, Glory was willing to pay it.

And now she walked barefoot, communing with the earth and spreading as much life magic as she could, sending it through the lands and sinking it deep into the watershed.

For days, she walked blindly, following where the pain led her.

It wasn't until their ninth day of walking that she

realized she was no longer trailing the Guardians of the Veil.

They were trailing her.

She blinked and glanced around. Mitaru pushed a piece of bread into her hand. "Here. Eat."

"Where are we?"

"I literally have no idea. All I know is that we're not too far off course. Kalina's keeping track of where we are in relation to Lawrence, Kansas."

"There's so much pain in this land. It makes me weep."

"I know." Mitaru looked unhappy. "I wanted to put you forcibly back on the horse, but Talvenia said to let you be, that this was part of your nature and it would be like trying to change the path of the wind. Was she right?"

"She was, yes. It's my magic, you see. It's linked to the magic of Faerie, intertwined really, but it's also linked to every living entity, pretty much everywhere. I can feel all of the Guardians. They're tired, but well. They're feeling hopeful, even though we've been cast out of Faerie.

"I can also feel my Guard. They're concerned that I'm going to exhaust myself, but as Talvenia said, they know to stop me would be impossible. My magic would constantly be reaching back out, trying to reconnect to the earth I'd been attempting to heal. To break the connection would be more harmful than good.

"I can feel the earth herself." She closed her eyes. "The river that runs a bit to the north of where we stand, the lake about forty miles to the west, the land that was screaming in agony an hour ago that is now quiet and soothed, a bit healthier, but not quite right yet." Her eyes flew open.

"There is a building the humans use to produce toxic chemicals. It's not far from the river and has contaminated everything around it. The land, the waters, the air, the humans, the animals, every living entity is suffering because of this one building. How do the humans not see what they're doing?"

"I don't know," Mitaru said.

"I've been infusing the land and the water with life magic. It's all I have to offer them. It won't be enough though, not so long as that building remains standing."

Mitaru cupped her face in his hands and kissed her gently. "Of course, it will be enough. You are the miracle this world and its mortals had no right to expect. If they choose not to take advantage of the miracle you offer them, that is on them, not you."

"Mitaru," Glory murmured, then kissed him back. "I'm so sorry I've not paid you much attention on this journey. I've been distracted."

"We'll have plenty of time for us, my love. For now, we do what we can for those who need us the most."

"And at the moment, it's these lands."

"Exactly." He kissed her again and this time, she allowed everything else to fade away until Mitaru was all that she could feel and smell and taste.

She shivered and wrapped her arms tighter around him, trying to get closer—

"Here now! That's enough of that!" Kalina and Thorne pulled the two of them apart and for a split second Glory imagined casting the two of them far from where they stood, perhaps down the shaft of the volcano just—

"You'll never guess who's here!" Kalina linked arms with Mitaru and dragged him away from Glory, leaving Thorne to grin at her and offer his arm gallantly.

Glory heaved a sigh, then accepted Thorne's arm and allowed him to escort her in Kalina's wake.

Glory's Guard, who had been standing a discreet distance away, followed.

"Several members of our unit have arrived," Kalina said to Mitaru.

"What do you mean?" Mitaru asked.

"Astra sent them after us. They arrived in these monster vehicles called buses. There are five of them and they say we can be in Kansas by mid-day tomorrow if we leave now."

"You've learned to drive?" Mitaru said incredulously to the newly arrived Guardians a few moments later.

"It's fun," the bright-eyed Guardian he had introduced as Jeniah exclaimed. "I didn't think I'd like it, but it's kind of like riding a horse."

"It's *nothing* like riding a horse," Yiveren, the Guardian at her side, said. "Don't listen to her. It *is* rather fun though."

"I was thinking to complete one last task before we leave," Glory said.

"Not a chance," Mitaru said.

"What?"

"I know exactly what you're thinking and we do not need that sort of trouble while we're out here vulnerable."

"That building needs to come down, Mitaru. It's killing people and wildlife and worse, it's killing the earth."

"I know, but have you looked around, Glory? There are buildings like that one everywhere. We need a better plan than to just destroy one building when the mortals will simply build a new one."

"Are you talking about the buildings the humans call factories and plants?" Jeniah asked.

"Plants?" Glory exclaimed. "Plants are full of life. These buildings suck the life out of the land around them. Why would the mortals call them plants? If anything, they are plant-killers."

"There is no understanding the mortals, I've decided," Zerika proclaimed.

"Isn't that the truth?" Mitaru muttered.

"Astra has a plan. We've been working hard to heal as much land as possible over the past year and we're making a difference, we really are," Jeniah said.

"Year?" Glory exclaimed. "Did you say year?"

"We knew time was paused while inside the shield," Mitaru said. "We just didn't realize how much time had actually passed."

"Well, it's actually been sixteen months since you three went inside the first time," Merina said.

"And more than eighteen months since the Veils fell," Toren said.

"I had no idea." Glory felt dazed. "Astra must have been so worried."

"We were all worried," Jeniah said. "I cried when Kalina and Thorne rode out of the mist and then again, when you and Mitaru did."

"When we rode out of the mist? You were there?"

"No. We watched it on the mortals' news station."

Glory didn't know what that was, but she was feeling overwhelmed enough that she decided not to ask. Instead, she brought them back to the previous conversation. "I don't feel right leaving that *factory* standing." She would never call such a thing a plant. It did not deserve the name.

"We can add it to our list," Jeniah said. "It's a long list of buildings that need to be replaced with something better. We don't have all the answers and it sometimes seems an impossible battle, but we're making progress little by little."

Glory sighed. She supposed she could wait then. After all, these Guardians from the West seemed to understand this world better than she did. It was probably best to defer to their knowledge, at least for now. "All right then. I guess we're moving out." She turned to face the many Guardians who hovered nearby. "Guardians, it's time for the final journey. These buses will take us to our new home."

After much discussion, they decided not to fly the banner of Faerie from the vehicles, but instead to try and travel incognito.

It had been impossible to hide their progress when walking. One hundred thirty-five Fae on foot weren't exactly subtle, especially as they walked through fields and across highways and down suburban roads.

The mortals had tried telling them they could not camp wherever they chose to stop, but the Fae had just ignored their protests and continued setting up camp wherever they chose.

After all, as far as Glory and the rest of the Fae were

concerned, the land belonged to no one and therefore was shelter for everyone.

This night, they had camped in a giant field, something the mortals had taken exception to, as it was something they called a baseball diamond.

Glory didn't know what a baseball was, but she knew this land was not a diamond.

It was also in pain, not as much as the lands around the factory, but enough that Glory didn't find it terribly soothing to camp there, but then none of the lands they walked across were that soothing.

The Guardians must have agreed with her because they were packed and boarding the buses within minutes.

Glory and Mitaru walked from bus to bus, double-checking at each one that no one from that bus's unit had been left behind. One by one, the buses pulled away.

Finally, they reached the last bus, where Kalina, Thorne and Nako were waiting.

"The Guardian unit on this bus is Nako's," Thorne said to Glory. "As you know I was transferred at the very last minute, to my great joy, to the Western Veil, where Kalina was serving. I thought it would be appropriate for all of us to travel with the unit I once served with. I hope that's okay."

Glory smiled at him. "It will be an honor to travel

with your original unit, Guardian Thorne, and with your current one, Guardian Nako."

And so, the final bus was boarded, first by Kalina, Thorne and Nako, then by half of Glory's Royal Guard, followed by Glory and Mitaru and the rest of her Guard.

The minute Glory reached the top of the stairs, the Guardians on board broke into cheers.

"We shall be celebrating your mating before you know it, Princess Glory!" One of the Guardians exclaimed, sheer delight on her face.

Glory smiled. "I'm so happy that we'll be able to celebrate it together." She touched a quick hand to the woman's shoulder, then moved toward the back of the bus, pausing to respond to comments along the way.

Finally, they settled at the back and Jeniah, who had requested the right to drive the bus that would transport the Princess, called out, "And we're off!"

With a rumble, the bus carrying Glory and Mitaru, Glory's Royal Guard, Thorne and Kalina, and Nako's Guardian unit of the Eastern Veil, pulled away from their last camping grounds and began the final phase of their long journey home.

CHAPTER 9

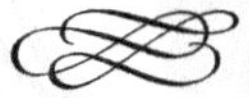

Glory woke with a start.

Everything felt different.

Everything.

She glanced around.

It was dark outside and everyone else on the bus was still sleeping.

She carefully extricated herself from Mitaru's arms, pausing a moment to brush a kiss across his cheek, before standing and making her way toward the front of the bus.

"Where are we?" she asked Jeniah.

"We just passed through the shield surrounding the western territories. We're in the state of Missouri, about four hours from Lawrence, Kansas, but at least now we're inside lands claimed by the magic of Faerie."

Yes.

That was it exactly.

The air felt cleaner.

The lands weren't crying out in pain, making her heart bleed.

Her throat wasn't quite so parched from the feel of the gritty, dying waters of the earth.

"Everything's healed here."

"Yes."

"I'm surprised Astra took this much land from the mortals."

"In the beginning, she just took a little, but the mortals kept demanding we return what little land we had taken, so she took a bit more, and then some more again. Then she got really angry, the more stories we heard from the indigenous tribes of the Americas.

"She said it would be one thing if the mortals had taken the lands and cared for them even half as well as the tribes did. Instead, they destroyed them.

"So she kept taking the lands back and giving them to the tribes who had lost them. Not that she's displaced anyone who's actually living on the lands. It was more symbolic than anything, putting the deeds for the lands in the names of the Indigenous Tribes."

"Wait. What do you mean, the tribes lost their lands? How does one lose a land?"

"They were taken from them by other mortals. The

Tribes were pushed into smaller patches of land far from their ancestral homes and they've been there ever since. There's a graphic online. It's quite distressing actually. Apparently, it barely took a hundred years to take ninety-nine percent of their lands away from the Tribes."

Glory was speechless. She had no idea what a graphic was or what it meant to be online, but she certainly understood the rest of what Jeniah was saying.

One hundred years to steal the land.

She wondered how many years it had taken the mortal thieves to destroy it, if it had taken them just as long or if they'd managed it in a fraction of that time.

"Good for Astra," she muttered, a fierce anger burning deep inside.

Jeniah gave a short nod. "Exactly what I said. Good for her."

Glory settled in the seat to the right of Jeniah and spoke with her softly as they traveled through the night.

A few hours later, she returned to the back of the bus where Mitaru was just starting to stir.

She settled into his arms again and together they stared out the back of the bus and watched the sun rise.

That same sun was high in the sky when Jeniah called out that they were approaching the secondary shield.

"There's a secondary shield?" Nako asked.

"There is," Jeniah said. "It surrounds the city of Lawrence. Actually, there's a Judicia Forest outside the city and it only allows in those it deems worthy. The secondary shield's a lot pickier than the tertiary one.

"There's a third shield now?" Thorne leaned forward to ask.

"There is. Astra has claimed quite a bit more land since you three have been gone."

"Did we already go through the tertiary shield then?" Mitaru wondered.

"We did," Jeniah said. "Several hours ago. You were all sound asleep. Anyway, the tertiary shield surrounds all of the territory Astra has claimed for the Fae. The secondary shield only surrounds the city of Lawrence."

"So what's the primary shield?" Nako wondered.

Jeniah threw a grin over their shoulder at them. "You'll see."

An hour later, they had made it through the Judicia Forest, a sight that took Glory's breath away.

She was simply amazed that Astra had managed such an incredible feat.

To grow a Judicia Forest, a true construct of Faerie, here in the mortal realm, was inconceivable and truly remarkable.

As they traveled through the town of Lawrence,

Glory noted that it did not resemble any mortal town she had seen to date.

The vegetation was incredible. Vines climbed the walls of buildings, making it appear as if those buildings were just a continuation of the forest they'd left behind.

The streets were made of cobblestone and dirt rather than the concrete the mortals seemed to favor and there were gardens everywhere.

"It's beautiful," Raiyana breathed.

"I did not expect this of the mortals," Talvenia said.

"I doubt this is the mortals' doing," Glory said. "This has Astra's magic written all over it. I wonder how the mortals feel about the transformation of this town."

Mitaru chuckled. "They seem happy enough." He pointed out the window and Glory saw that he was right.

Children were playing in what appeared to be a miniature forest maze that wove in and out of a community garden.

Laughter rang through the air.

"That's a lovely sight," Xilarin said. "It has been entirely too long since I have seen children at play."

This was the dark side of being such a long-lived species. The longer one lived, the greater the distance between those who were young and innocent and the one who had seen centuries of life.

That distance grew until often there was no innocence left even in the periphery of an adult Fae's life.

Glory caught her breath as she felt a pull on her magic. A quick glance around told her everyone else had felt it as well.

"That must have been the primary shield," Nako said. "I didn't even notice it until we were through it."

"By the fates," one of the Guardians exclaimed. "Is that a castle?"

"It sure is!" Jeniah called out.

"It's gotten a lot bigger since we left," Kalina said.

"Yes, well, wait until you see it up close. The minute we knew you were headed here with so many more Guardians, we started expanding it."

"It looks like it's made of vines," Nako said.

"That's because it is," Jeniah said. "It's made entirely of the living earth. There are gardens everywhere, inside and out, and you're just going to love it. It's kind of crazy outside the shield, but here inside it, we have the next best thing to Faerie itself."

Silence fell as everyone watched the castle get closer.

"It's beautiful," another of the Guardians murmured.

She was right.

The castle was simply breathtaking.

The walls appeared to be made from tightly woven, flowering vines. There were long walkways connecting corner towers and a huge courtyard that looked like something out of one of those fairy tales Thorne had been talking about.

"And we're here!" The rumble of the bus engine died as Jeniah turned to grin at them. "Well, come on. It's time to see your new home!" She opened the door and led the way down the steps.

The Guardians in the bus all turned to look at Glory.

She smiled back at them. "Go ahead. We'll be right behind you."

It took several minutes for everyone to get off the bus.

The Guardians of the Eastern Veil exited first, followed by Nako, Thorne and Kalina, then by Glory's Royal Guard.

Mitaru pulled Glory to her feet, threaded his fingers through hers and together they followed her Guard down the aisle toward their new life together.

CHAPTER 10

"I don't see her, Kahji. I don't see her." Astra couldn't keep the anxiety from her voice.

"Yiveren assured you she's on the final one and there it is." Kahji pointed toward the bus that was just then making the turn into the small parking lot the Fae had constructed from stone when Astra had finally come to terms with everything she needed to do to ensure the Fae didn't just survive, but that they thrived in their new world.

First on that list had been the need to acquire a better mode of transportation than the few horses they'd had at the time. It still hadn't been enough. She'd had to trade entirely too many favors for the use of three additional buses to bring her Guardians home.

Still, looking around at the parking lot that was now filled with Guardians anxiously awaiting the last of their brethren, the cost of those favors was a small price to pay.

Especially when it also brought her sister home that much faster.

Astra bounced up on and down on the balls of her feet, anxious to see Glory at long last. "Come on, Kahji. Let's get closer." She dragged him through the crowd.

"Fine." Kahji laughed. "Just remember—she's not going to be the first one off the bus. In fact, I would imagine she'll probably be the last one off. Her Royal Guard will insist upon it."

"Yes, yes, I know." Astra watched anxiously as the doors opened and Jeniah stepped through them.

Jeniah turned and everyone waited for a long moment before the final unit of the Guardians of the Eastern Veil began to descend the steps.

They moved away from the bus, greeting friends who waited them, then turned to watch with everyone else as first, Talvenia, the Captain of Glory's Royal Guard, and then the rest of her Guard, stepped out one by one.

As they exited, they formed a double line facing each other on either side of the door, creating an Honor Guard for Glory.

Astra grinned.

Glory would hate that. She wasn't one to stand on ceremony unless it was to make a point, like she had with the mortals.

Here, among the Fae, though—

Yep.

Astra giggled as Glory appeared in the doorway and rolled her eyes at her Royal Guard.

Glory must have heard Astra's laugh because her head jerked up and she scanned the crowd.

Astra was already moving when Glory caught sight of her and darted forward as well.

The Honor Guard was a complete waste since Glory was through it in a flash, flinging herself into Astra's arms.

They came together in an explosion of relief and tears, clutching each other close, trying to share everything they had missed, but entirely too excited to be anything but incoherent.

Finally, with a laugh, they pulled back and simply smiled at each other.

Glory looked absolutely stunning to Astra's eyes, not at all like she'd been missing for eighteen months. "You're not hurt?"

Glory shook her head. "We were all frozen behind the shield. Basically, my magic put us all to sleep."

Astra thought she should probably be surprised, but she was entirely too relieved to feel anything else.

"You're safe too?" Glory asked. "No injuries?"

Astra shook her head. "I'm fine. Oh, but I'm mated." She reached back and grabbed Kahji's hand and pulled him forward.

For a moment, Glory looked stunned, then a look of pure fury crossed her face. "Is this a joke? He denied you were mates for *a thousand years!*"

Astra winced. That probably hadn't been the best way to break the news to Glory. She should have led up to it slowly.

"That was the worst mistake of my life, Princess Glory," Kahji said. "I thought I was protecting the princess, that I wasn't worthy of her."

Glory scowled. "Rest assured, you were right. You are *not* worthy of her."

"Glory!" Astra gasped.

"He made you think you weren't mates, Astra, sent you searching elsewhere for something you would never find. He made you wait a *thousand* years. And now he suddenly decides he wants to claim you?"

Astra grinned. "Believe me, I made him work for it."

"She did," Kahji agreed.

Glory glared at him. "If you *ever* make her cry again the way she did on her hundredth birthday, I will *eviscerate* you."

Astra glanced up in time to see Kahji's jaw tighten. She knew it was because he did not like to be reminded of how much he had hurt her.

"You would be well within your rights," he said. "I shall devote my life to making things right with her *and* her family."

Glory was silent for a long moment, studying Kahji, before she finally said, "All right, then. You've got one chance and one chance only. Do *not* let my sister down."

She smiled at Astra. "And on that note, I have news as well." She reached behind her and grabbed Mitaru's hand.

Astra hadn't even noticed him standing there.

Glory pulled him to her side. "I've found my mate."

"Mitaru's your mate?" Astra exclaimed. "This is wonderful!" She'd spent the last eighteen months feeling so guilty about sending the Guardians east. She'd been grateful only three of them had managed to penetrate the shield, but also sick with worry and guilt that they hadn't made it out again.

Knowing that Mitaru was Glory's mate relieved some of that guilt. He was probably meant to be there all along, to help Glory regain control of her magic, which was no doubt how he'd managed to break through the shield in the first place. Kalina and Thorne had probably only been allowed in because of the bonds the three shared between them.

"Congratulations!" Astra beamed at her sister and Mitaru. She was so happy for each of them, she couldn't say whom she was more delighted for in that moment.

"Thanks," Glory said. "Any chance we can have our celebration this evening? I've made Mitaru wait long enough, I think."

"You waited to celebrate with us?" Astra gave a hop of excitement. "This is fabulous. We're going to have a mating celebration!" She shouted.

Cheers and clapping erupted around them as Guardians from both the Western and Eastern Veils shared a moment of pure joy.

The sun was just beginning to set when Glory faced Mitaru in front of huge crowds of Fae and mortals alike.

She'd expected the Guardians to attend, if only because Mitaru was one of them. She'd also expected, of course, that her sister and Kahji would attend, plus both their Royal Guards, but word had spread throughout the afternoon that a Royal mating ceremony was about to take place.

It was Fae tradition to travel long distances for

mating ceremonies and for a Royal ceremony, that was doubly true.

Glory simply hadn't realized how many Fae were locked on the mortal side of the Veils until they began arriving in droves for her mating ceremony.

Even more astonishing was the joy with which they greeted her, even though she knew their hearts were bleeding for all they had lost and left behind in Faerie.

During those eighteen months Glory had been sleeping, Astra had apparently been building strong bonds with the indigenous communities and other mortals.

As a result, they, too, arrived to celebrate her sister's mating.

And so the mating took place near a lake on the land Astra had claimed, right beside the primary shield so that mortals could bear witness as well.

"Glory." Mitaru held her hands in his, stared into her eyes and spoke his vows with a firm voice. ""I see eternity in your eyes and no matter the length of our days, I shall know peace so long as you are by my side. I offer you everything that I am, everything that I have been and everything I've yet to become, in this realm and in any other, in this lifetime and in all the rest. With you, *for* you, Glory, I am my best self."

Glory was a Fae princess, and as such, was used to

having many eyes upon her at all times. She was used to giving speeches and even to serving justice when needed, but this, standing in front of crowds of both mortals and Fae, pledging her life and love to her mate, something so intimate it made her heart squeeze, was an entirely different beast.

She could barely find her voice now that it was time to speak her vows in return.

She had to clear her throat twice before she could made herself be heard. "Mitaru, my love, I see eternity in your eyes and no matter the length of our days, I shall know peace so long as you are by my side. I offer you everything that I am, everything that I have been and everything I've yet to become, in this realm and in any other, in this lifetime and in all the rest."

She took a deep breath, the feeling of pressure easing as she finished with a song in her heart. "With you, *for* you, Mitaru, I am my best self."

A thousand blessings be upon this mating. It was Queen Naira's voice that offered the blessing, but the words seemed to come from everywhere, from the trees and the wind that swept through them, from the lake and the waters that shifted within it, from the grass beneath their feet and the clouds in the sky above.

Glory's eyes teared up to hear her mother's voice, offering the traditional blessing for her mating.

Queen Naira was still in Faerie, far from her daughters, yet somehow she managed to be there with Glory in this moment, to share with her and Mitaru their greatest joy.

Glory lost herself in Mitaru's eyes, her heart singing with joy, as Queen Naira's magic rained down upon them in tiny sparks of power, a royal blessing from Faerie that set their matebond aflame.

Glory was reaching for Mitaru when Astra swept her away. "Time to celebrate!"

And so the hours passed as tradition dictated, with Glory and Mitaru dancing, never quite together, but never too far apart, either, celebrating with their many friends, dancing long into the night.

Every once in a while, one of the Fae would whirl Glory into Mitaru's arms and he would kiss her until they were both burning with need, then some other Fae would separate them again and the dancing would continue.

And so the night flew by, time measured in the occasional brush of a hand or a flaming hot kiss, a sweet caress as they strained toward each other even as their partners whirled them apart.

It was only when the skies lightened as the darkest of night gave way to the approaching dawn that Glory and Mitaru were finally able to sneak away.

He led her deep into the palace, up some stairs and

down a long corridor to a room at the back of the palace that overlooked the gardens.

Glory had a moment to think she might enjoy exploring those gardens with Mitaru, then he had her in his arms and was kissing her while carrying her through the open doors and down the stairs that led into the gardens beyond.

He carried her through the garden, kissing her still, and then they were falling.

He twisted as they fell, so that she landed on top. She glanced around and saw that they had landed on a bed made entirely of flowers and leaves and branches.

"Kalina, Thorne and the rest of the Guardians put this together for us," Mitaru murmured. "It is their way of blessing our union."

Mitaru.

Mitaru's eyes widened. *Glory, my love. It seems I have waited an eternity to hear your voice inside me.*

I was afraid to speak with you like this until now. I thought if I heard your voice, I might not be able to wait for our mating ceremony.

Mitaru grinned. *In that case, it was well worth the wait, my love.* He pulled her down for a kiss, plunging his tongue deep, then rolling them so that he was on top.

He reared back and ripped his tunic off, then leapt from the bed to pull her to her feet. He stripped her gown from her in an economy of movement, then froze at the sight of her.

She smiled and stepping forward, placed her hands on his shoulders, leaned up and nibbled along his jawline.

He let out a groan, then pulled her close and kissed her.

The feel of his skin against hers made Glory whimper. She strained closer to him, trying to somehow crawl inside him.

Her skin prickled as heat ran up and down her spine, flames rippling everywhere. *Mitaru, please.*

He let out another groan, then lifted her closer.

She wrapped her legs around his waist and squirmed.

He moved them back to the bed, where he leaned over and settled her on it. He tried to stand, but she came with him, holding tight, not wanting to let him go.

Glory, my love, just give me one moment. One moment.

It took her that long just to understand he wanted her to let him go so that he could finish removing his clothes.

After a few false starts, she managed to unclench her arms and legs long enough for him to strip away his trousers.

She barely had time to miss him before he was back, settling over her and kissing her thoroughly.

Mitaru.

Glory, my love. He caught her hands in his, clasped their fingers together, and sank deep.

Then there were no more thoughts, just the feel of Mitaru. He was everywhere, surging deep, plunging in and out, making her gasp for breath.

She lunged upward and buried her face in his neck, inhaled his scent and whimpered. *Mitaru, please. I need, I burn.*

Ah, my sweet love. He pulled back, then surged forward, then back again, only to plunge deep once more.

The heat ratcheted up, again and again, until she could barely breathe through the flames.

Glory.

Mitaru!

Glory flung back her head, eyes blind to the world around her as everything was erased in a great ball of white fire that consumed them both.

Mitaru could barely breathe in the aftermath. "I think you've killed me, my love," he rasped out.

Glory giggled. "But what a way to walk into eternity, am I right?"

"Oh, you're definitely right, and if you give me another thirty minutes or so, I'll walk you into eternity again."

I can hardly wait, my love.

"Well, that did it." Mitaru lunged up and settled over Glory again.

"What? How is that even possible?"

"You spoke. That is all."

Glory was still giggling when he sank deep and somehow their second round ended up being even more exceptional than the first.

Yep. Killing me.

The week that followed was indescribable. Someone delivered food to their rooms every day, but they never saw anyone at all.

Mitaru and Glory spent their days exploring the

private gardens outside their room and celebrating their mating in every corner of them.

They then spent their nights indulging in more celebrations of the same. They ate to keep up their strength and they spent hours upon hours just talking.

They had learned much about each other in the days they had traveled from D.C. to Lawrence, but there was still so much more to learn.

They shared endless stories of their pasts with each other, Glory of growing up a Royal with three older brothers and an older sister, Mitaru of caring for his much younger sisters, Luna and Zara.

I hope I can meet them someday, she murmured late one night, while sprawled across his chest, tracing the markings of a Guardian that wandered there.

He knew who she meant, of course, though they hadn't spoken of Luna or Zara that day. *I hope so as well. I pray to the fates and to Faerie herself that they are well in my absence, that they do not mourn too much and that they find their happiness as I have found my own.*

Mitaru, my love. If they are half as sweet as you, the fates would never deny them their due.

Mitaru grinned and flipped them over so that he was now looking down at her. "Their due? Is that what you think? That because I am sweet, the Fates owed me you?"

"But of course. And look here. You have me, so I must be right."

He chuckled. "I do have you, that is true. So that being the case, perhaps I should take my due again. What say you?"

Glory laughed. "I say, take what you will, my love. All that I am, all that I will ever be, is yours."

Ah, my love, my Glorious darling due, I think I shall. With that, he kissed her breathless and there were no more words spoken for quite some time.

Mitaru's sisters are up next!

LUNA and ZARA, have been left behind in Faerie. Read on for an excerpt from Luna's story in THE VEILED.

$\mathcal{L}$UNA VERUSHI GLARED at the arrogant Fae who seemed to think he could boss her around just because he was having a crisis over the fact they were mates.

Not that he'd acknowledged their bond or anything.

Oh, no, he'd been too busy lecturing her to bother with something as important as a mating.

Which was absolutely fine with her.

She didn't need a mate and certainly not one who thought he knew what was best for her.

"You're not going," he growled for what had to be the seventh time since he'd knocked on her lodging's door that morning.

She didn't even know his name because he hadn't bothered to introduce himself.

Instead, he'd taken one look at her and started ranting about staying behind and letting him handle the situation.

As if he even knew what the situation was.

Beyond what everyone in Faerie already knew, of course—that the Veils had fallen, then reformed as solid barriers, no longer open for travel between the realms. In the process, thousands of Fae had been trapped on the mortal side of the Veils, cut off entirely from Faerie.

Beyond that, he shouldn't even know that she had a plan—no matter that it was a rather risky one—let alone the specifics of it. Even more perplexing was how he'd managed to find her in the first place.

There was only one other person who knew what Luna had discovered and surely she wouldn't—

Luna whirled and glared at the interfering Fae. "Did Zara send you?"

He stopped ranting and faced her, eyebrow raised. "Do you honestly believe she should have just let you carry on with your reckless plan on your own, with no backup? Is that what you think?"

Luna rolled her eyes. "It isn't reckless. I've done all the calculations and I have the entire natural world to back me up."

"Look, I'm sure you're quite talented, but in the mortal world, you cannot possibly expect to retain full access to whatever tiny bits of earth magic you happen to have here in Faerie."

Luna gasped. "Tiny bits of earth magic? Why you—" She barely caught the reins of her magic as it surged in reaction to her fury.

No.

He wasn't worth expelling the energy to teach him a lesson, no matter how tempting it was.

She whirled around, grabbed the last of her things, shoved them into her satchel and closed it tight.

Swinging it over her shoulder, she headed for the door.

"And just where do you think you're going?" He followed her out of her room and down the stairs into the main room of the inn where she'd been staying.

She ignored him because honestly, she did not need this additional stress on the morning of her grand adventure.

She already had no idea how this trip would go— whether she would make it to her intended destination and even if she did, whether she would ever be able to return.

Perhaps she'd be trapped just like the many other missing Fae.

Worst case scenario, she'd be trapped somewhere far from her brother.

Best case, she'd find him quickly and at least be with part of her family while cut off from Faerie.

Because of its unpredictability and inherent risks, this entire adventure had her anxiety soaring, especially since Zara had been called away at the last minute to assist in a royal healing, leaving Luna to make this trip on her own.

She would have waited for Zara, but Luna had been tracking this roaming Veil all over Faerie for an entire year, and somehow she always managed to just barely miss it.

She couldn't afford to skip this opportunity, even knowing she'd probably fail again, because there was always the possibility that her calculations were actually correct this time and she would arrive at the perfect moment.

It was actually a bit of a terrifying thought—that she might, by the vagaries of fate, catch the Veil the one time Zara wasn't with her, and would have no choice but to take the risk and travel through it alone.

Zara had to know that Luna wouldn't wait and risk missing the Veil again, which was probably why she'd sent to Luna this infuriating, overbearing, condescending Fae, who was full of arrogant assumptions and a ridiculous belief that he could dictate her actions.

Worse yet was the fact that he turned out to be her mate.

Fate could be such a vindictive, hateful creature sometimes.

"Are you even listening to me?"

Luna didn't answer. It wasn't worth attempting to reason with him as he obviously lacked the logic gene.

She stormed out of the inn and set off down the path toward the woods where her window of opportunity was winding down.

"You need to stop and think, Luna," the Fae insisted as he followed her. "This isn't safe. If you wish for someone to test your theory, I will happily do so. It would be an honor, but you cannot do this yourself. You are of Faerie and you need to remain here. We cannot risk the loss of yet another—"

"Another what? Female?" She continued down the path, refusing to pause for even a moment to address his outrageous claims. "There are plenty of females trapped on the wrong side of the Veils and I'm going to find them and help them come home if they wish."

"It isn't your job, Luna —"

"Stop saying my name as if you know who I am."

"I know exactly who you are. You are Zara's little sister and the youngest sister of Mitaru, a Guardian trapped in the mortal realm when the Veils fell."

"Congratulations. That tells you exactly nothing." She brushed some branches aside as she entered the woods and began to run, a feeling of urgency creeping upon her, as if the window was closing faster than she'd expected.

"I can assure you, Mitaru would not thank me for allowing his baby sister to take such risks."

"Mitaru would support me as he always did and he would trust me. Do not speak as if you know anything of our relationship." She practically flew down the path, furious that he continued to follow her, arguing the entire way.

"Very well then. I'll speak of what I know of our relationship instead. You are my mate, Luna." The Fae kept pace with her as he spoke emphatically of a mating she now wanted no part of.

"Good luck with that one." She raced faster and faster, leaping over obstacles, the beacon calling her ramping up in power.

"Luna, please, listen to me."

They burst into a clearing and Luna stumbled to a halt.

There it was.

The roaming Veil that she'd been tracking for a year.

Her last hope.

"Finally," she whispered.

"It's even smaller than I expected," the Fae murmured at her side.

She'd almost forgotten he was there.

"How in the name of Faerie are you planning to breach it?"

She shrugged. "The Sorenalaya never seem to have any trouble."

"Because they're insubstantial. They can squeeze through the tiniest pinprick. We, however, are made of flesh and bone and could never fit through that minuscule portion of the Veil."

"Not we. Me."

"Absolutely not. If you think I'm going to allow—"

"Excuse me? You're insane if you think you can dictate anything to me." She pushed her other arm through the second strap of her satchel, settling it more firmly on her back, and focused on the spaces to either side of the Veil. "I suggest you stand back."

Whatever he was going to say was lost in the rumble that began beneath their feet, the land lifting and subsiding in a great wave that split into two directions and ended about three feet to the left and right of the minuscule, roaming Veil.

Everything fell to stillness, then in the quiet, two bushes sprang to life on either side of the Veil.

Rising from the ground, they went from brown to green to fully abloom in purple and white flowers in a fraction of an instant.

The tiny pocket of space that had broken free from the Veils' countless years before, that had not been impacted by their fall or their reformation as closed gateways, reacted immediately.

It began to turn and twist until it faced both bushes at the same time, then reached toward them, a tiny pocket in space stretching and growing until it became a narrow window through which Luna planned to travel.

The Fae's jaw dropped. "How did you do that?"

"I left instructions for my sister on the table in my house in case I do not return. See that she gets them, would you?" With that, Luna took a running leap and dove headfirst through the roaming Veil.

At the very last second, something caught her ankle on the Faerie side, but her momentum was so great it simply pulled whatever had hold of her through the Veil with her.

Luna landed in a heap on the mortal side, stunned to find herself lying on her back when logic dictated she should have landed on her stomach.

Twisty, tricky roaming Veil to somehow turn her entire body—or perhaps it turned the world—and leave her blinking at the stars in the sky above, pinned under the weight of an obnoxious, overbearing Fae who had somehow latched on and traveled with her.

Shoving him off her, she scrambled up and was gratified to realize, after a quick glance around in the darkness lit only by the light of the stars and moon, that there were no mortals in their vicinity. "I cannot believe you! The least you can do is give me your name before deciding to stalk me through the Veil."

The Fae lunged to his feet and sketched a sweeping bow in her direction. "Tarek Evaria, at your service." He held the position for a long moment, making Luna's breath catch in her throat as his dark eyes remained on hers.

Dragging in a deep breath, she took another giant step backward while attempting to shake off the effects of his compelling gaze. "Look, Tarek, I did not ask for you to be at my service so don't—"

"Luna," Tarek said, straightening quickly, eyes wide. "Stop moving."

"For Fae's sake! Is every word out of your mouth a command? Have you never heard the word please? Or perhaps a 'Would you consider?' That would be a nice change—to be asked instead of commanded."

"Seriously, just step toward me." He reached out an arm and beckoned her closer.

Luna threw her hands in the air. "It's like I'm talking to air." She moved to step back again and Tarek lunged forward, catching her with a pop of air magic that flung her into his arms with such force, they both ended up on the ground again.

This time, she was on top. "Are you insane?"

"What kind of idiotic Fae lands in another world

and doesn't even bother to take in her surroundings?" Tarek lunged to his feet, hauling her up with him in a massive display of strength that made her heart hammer in her chest.

"Well, excuse me. It happens to be a little dark out here!" She must have miscalculated the timing as she'd expected to arrive mid-morning. Instead, the sun had not yet risen. Either that or it was the roaming Veil again, not just twisting the world when they traveled through it, but twisting time too.

Tarek moved away from where she'd been standing, then set her on her feet and whirled her around so she stood with her back to his chest. "That should have just made you take more care, especially when you knew we'd be landing here!" He swept an arm out to encompass the view in front of them.

Luna's breath caught in her throat. "The canyon of the tribes," she whispered and wondered if the Havasupai and others still made their homes there.

A glance around showed her they'd landed on a ledge, the majestic wall of the canyon rising at their back, a path on their left leading up while another to their right headed down, and directly across, mere steps from where they'd originally landed, the cavernous canyon of the tribes stretched before them.

Tarek was right.

It might be dark out, but it certainly wasn't pitch

black. The sky had enough light that dawn couldn't be far off, meaning she should never have missed the canyon she'd almost backed into, not that she would ever admit that to Tarek.

Besides, if he hadn't insisted on joining her, she'd never have been distracted or trying to back away from him in the first place.

In other words, this was definitely his fault.

"You see?" he demanded.

Luna rolled her eyes at the superior tone in his voice. Then, just to aggravate him, she gave a quick hop of excitement and squealed, "I do see! Can you believe it? I've only ever been here once before—and that was hundreds of years ago—but it was so majestic, I've always wanted to come back. I cannot believe the roaming Veil brought us here."

"Hold on a minute. Are you saying you didn't even know where we'd end up when you went through the Veil?" Tarek demanded incredulously.

"Of course, I didn't know. No one knows where a Veil like that will lead. They're completely unpredictable, hopping around, visiting different places. That's why they're called roaming Veils." She'd never have thought she'd be grateful for their unpredictability, yet here she was, profoundly grateful to be at this site once more.

"What kind of idiot dives through a tiny pocket in

space without knowing where they'll land?" Tarek exploded behind her. "Are you insane? We could have both ended up falling to our deaths!"

Luna whirled to face him, hands on her hips. "Well, no one invited you, you pompous hitchhiker!"

"Excuse me? What in the world is a hitchhiker?"

Luna threw her arms up and stomped past him, intending to leave him behind, but his accusations rang in her head, goading her past endurance. "And another thing!" She whirled to face him again. "What kind of idiot comes into the mortal world dressed like that?" She waved an arm at his ridiculous garb.

"What are you talking about?"

"You look Fae!"

"I am Fae."

"Yes, and now you're obviously Fae in the mortal realm!"

"What's your point?"

"My point is you need to look mortal."

"Why in the name of Faerie would I want that?"

She just stared at him.

"We are the immortal Fae! Do you honestly believe the mortals are a threat? To us? Besides, we can just use our glamour."

"First of all, even mortals can be a threat in significant enough numbers, Tarek. Secondly, the mortal world has changed in ways we cannot even imagine.

Thousands of Fae crossed over in a moment. It's completely illogical to assume the mortals witnessed none of the crossings and that our glamour will still work on those witnesses. Witnesses who have now seen the truth."

Tarek let out a huff of exasperation. "You know as well as I do, Luna, that the mortals excel at burying their heads in the sand. I'm sure within moments, they had a logical explanation for the crossing and it's doubtful that explanation had anything to do with the Fae."

"That's a really big leap in logic. Besides, it bears repeating—in significant enough numbers, anything can become a threat. And in this case, those numbers, at least to the mortals, were the Fae appearing out of nowhere. So, assuming you want to survive this trip, we need to be traveling incognito—thank goodness no one was around to see our arrival—which means you're just going to have to look the part, like I do. Time to Veil your Fae–ness." With that, she waved a hand and the threads holding together Tarek's very traditional, Fae clothing unraveled.

Find out what happens next in THE VEILED.

THE MURRYSVILLE COALITION

The Crazy Cheetah Lady

One Sad Kitty

A PAWSITIVELY PURRFECT MATCH

Catnapped

The Real McCat

Unbearably Cute

A Catmas to Remember

This Cat's for You

Santa Kitty

Hocus Purrcus

Tridents & Tails

Abra-Cat-Abra

Satan's Kitty

Valen-Cats

Vampurr Lovin'

A Beautiful Cat-ship

Grave Cattitude

THE SHENANIGANS SERIES

Shifter Shenanigans

Witchy Shenanigans

Full Moon Shenanigans

Hotel Shenanigans

Dragon Shenanigans

Undercover Shenanigans

Spooky Shenanigans

Holiday Shenanigans

Valentine Shenanigans

Lucky Shenanigans

STORIES OF THE VEIL

Guardians of the Veil

Astra

Glory

Luna

Zara

WICKED

No Rest for the Wicked

Wicked Is As Wicked Does

ANTHOLOGIES & COLLECTIONS

PAWSITIVELY PURRFECT TRILOGIES

THE CAT'S MEOW

Catnapped | The Real McCat | Unbearably Cute

HOLLY JOLLY PAWLIDAY

A Catmas to Remember | This Cat's for You | Santa Kitty

SHENANIGANS ANTHOLOGIES

CRAZED

Books 1-3

AMAZED

Books 4-6

HOLIDAZED

Books 7-10

SHENANIGANS

The Complete Collection

STORIES OF THE VEIL

THE UNVEILED

Astra | Glory

THE VEILED

Luna | Zara

WICKED DUET

WICKED

No Rest for the Wicked | Wicked Is As Wicked Does

ABOUT THE AUTHOR

WWW.PEPPERMCGRAW.COM

PEPPER MCGRAW is a *USA Today* Bestselling Author of paranormal romance. She hasn't met any paranormals to date, but she's sure that moment is just around the corner!

Pepper loves animals, especially cats, and spends her free time volunteering at local shelters and for Trap-Neuter-Release programs.

She's had the supreme honor of winning occasional head butts and meows from the local ferals in her neighborhood and has even convinced a few to come inside and adopt her as their own.

BB bookbub.com/authors/pepper-mcgraw

f facebook.com/ShenanigansSeries

g goodreads.com/peppermcgraw

instagram.com/peppermcgraw_author

tiktok.com/@peppermcgraw

twitter.com/peppermcgraw